DANGEROUS PASSIONS

DANGEROUS VISIONS

DANGEROUS PASSIONS

LEIGH ANDERSON

Red Empress Publishing
www.RedEmpressPublishing.com

ALSO BY LEIGH ANDERSON

Urban Fantasy

Pirate's Curse

Sword Kissed

Gothic Romance

The Creation of Eve

Dangerous Passions

The Sumerian Curse

The Vampire's Daughter

PART I

"*The dreams we imagine when we are asleep should not in any way make us doubt the truth of the thoughts we have when we are awake.*"

~Descartes

CHAPTER ONE

"*I*soline..."

Isoline gasped as she opened her eyes. He was here...again...always...

"*Isoline...*"

She climbed out of bed, her hands gripping her satin robe as she stood, but when she looked back, the bed was gone, as were the walls of her room. She wrapped the robe around herself as the fog crept in around her ankles. She was somewhere outside. She could feel the grass under her feet and the dampness in the air, yet she was not cold. The strange sensations told her that none of this was real...yet she knew it was.

"*Isoline...*" he called to her again.

"I'm here," she replied softly. "Show yourself." She knew he would not, but still she tried to convince him to reveal his face. In the five years he had been coming to her in her dreams, she had not seen who he was, but she could feel he had gotten closer to her.

She took a step forward. Just because she was alone in a dream with a strange man did not mean she could not enjoy a short walk. She had been coming here for so long, this place no longer terrified her.

It was a large open glade, with grass up to her knees, surrounded by forest. She had tried many times to reach the edge of the glade, but she had never made it that far. A pale blue moon lighted her way. She clutched tightly to the robe at her chest and ran the tips of her fingers along the edges of the grass as she walked. She shivered, not from cold, but from the way the grass tickled her bare calves as she walked.

She heard footsteps behind her. She slowly turned her head, but there was no one there, as usual. She continued her walk, and she heard the footsteps again, closer this time.

"I want to see you," she said. "It is time, don't you think?"

He did not respond, but she felt the wind lightly touch the ends of her long dark hair. No...it wasn't the wind. It was him. She knew it was. She shivered again.

"If you cannot reveal yourself to me you need to stop bringing me here," she said. "I..." She had delayed in telling him the truth. This man in her dreams. She shook her head, disappointed with herself. What was she afraid of? Offending a figment of her imagination?

But what she knew to be true and what she knew to be reasonable and logical warred in her mind. She knew she was dreaming. But she also knew this was much more than a dream. But if it was more than a dream, what was it? It was the unknown that scared her more than the dream itself. She no longer feared the dream as she once did. She actually longed for it. She did not know what caused the dreams to happen. There seemed to be no logical order to when they happened. One night, two nights, three nights could pass before she would find herself here. When too many nights passed that she was not awakened by him calling her name, she would miss him. Miss this place.

And yet, as a dream, she could not let it stop her from living.

But she did. She had for too long. She had to put an end to it. It was time to focus on the world of the waking.

"I am getting married," she finally said in one quick breath.

The world stilled. For the first time in a dream, she felt cold. She pulled her robe more tightly around her and could see the crystals of her own breath before her.

"Do not be angry," she said. "You know we cannot continue like this."

We. As if she had a choice in being here. She could not will the dreams to come to her. She had tried. She could not change the content of the dreams. She had tried that as well. And yet...she wanted to be here. She wanted to see this man who had called to her all these years. She wanted to know him. To touch him. To see him. But if he could not give her that, she could not keep coming here.

"It is dishonorable to my future husband," she said. "I cannot keep coming to you from my marriage bed. It is disloyal."

From over her shoulder, she could see him breathing. He was right behind her. Her own breath stilled. They were so close. If only she could touch him.

"Just show me your face," she panted, "and I will end the engagement."

The hairs on her arms prickled. He was right there, so close. Almost touching her but not quite. She had to look. She turned to face him.

And he was gone.

She stood alone in the field.

"Who are you?" she yelled.

*I*soline opened her eyes. She felt near to tears. Was that it? Was he gone? Was it over? She sat up and shook her head. She needed to get ready for the day. She pulled the covers back and shivered as her feet touched the ground. Her warming pan had long gone cold, but her down blanket provided immeasurable warmth compared to the chilly room, her fire nearly gone out. She pulled on some woolen socks and a thick fur-lined robe. She crept over to her fireplace and tossed some more logs on it. Her family had some servants, but not enough to tend to every single need. The family was comfortably upper-middle class, but not wealthy. Of course, her father hoped that her marriage to Lord Crowden would change their circumstances. And she did as well. She found Cyril pleasant enough of a companion and could imagine loving him one day. It was a good match, she had to agree.

He was no man from her dreams, though.

She removed the kettle from over the fireplace and added the water to the nearly frozen water in her washbowl to make it a comfortable temperature. She washed and selected her own clothes for the day, dressing herself as completely as she could before the maid, Nicola, arrived to help her tie and fasten everything she couldn't reach.

"You look pretty as a picture today, Miss Beresford," Nicola gushed as she helped Isoline tame her wild tresses into something like an acceptable hairstyle. "Of course, your father would accept nothing less on the day of your engagement party."

Isoline felt her heart skip a beat at Nicola's words. It didn't hardly seem real to her, not yet. Cyril had only proposed two days previously. She had accepted, not because she loved him, but because it had been the right thing to do. Cyril Hawtree, Lord Crowden, was a baron with a proper house and medium-sized estate only a few miles from her home in the village of Hawkshire. He was reasonably handsome, with fair hair and grey eyes, and only in his early thirties. He was more than ten years older than Isoline, but that was preferable to the other landed gentry her father would surely consider if she waited much longer to find a husband on her own. She was not an old maid, or even anything like it, but any woman who had been in society for five years would soon surely be on borrowed time.

It wasn't that men had not been interested in her when she was younger, but she had not been interested in them. In her foolish, girlhood days, she had given much more power, more credence to her dreams. She imagined the man calling to her was going to simply breeze through the doors one day and sweep her away to a life of magic and passion.

But nothing of the sort had happened, and Isoline liked to think she had grown a little wiser, in addition to older. She was not sure what her dreams meant, if anything, or what the source was. But five years was long enough to wait for any man. And she was done waiting.

Nicola finished dressing Isoline by adding a simple pearl necklace and pearl drop earrings. "There, my lovely. Your mother must surely be smiling down on you today."

Isoline touched the pearls at her throat and couldn't help but notice the similarity between herself and her mother. The same dark eyes and hair, the same pale skin, the same nose and ears. She had died when Isoline was fifteen, the year before she started having the dreams. She hoped her mother would be proud of the woman she had become.

Isoline took a deep breath, nodded, and headed downstairs.

The house was a flurry of activity. All of the staff, as well as her brothers and sisters-in-law, had been tasked with preparing for the party that evening. Compared to Lord Crowden's estate, their house was quite simple. It took a lot of work—and money—to bring it up to the standards of the class of people who would be attending tonight to give the soon-to-be bride and groom their well-wishes.

She only had time for a bit of toast and tea before she was whisked away to help arrange the flowers and rearrange the furniture. Gifts and notes arrived in a steady stream. And lording over all of it, was Isoline's father, Vincent Beresford.

"All of this must be moved *out* of the room," he barked at a footman. "I don't care if there isn't any space, drag it upstairs if you must!"

"Papa, you are going to give yourself an aneurysm if you don't calm down," Isoline said as she held a door open wide enough for the poor footmen to move an awkward over-stuffed chair from the room, doing her best to lighten the mood with a smile.

"As long as you are married before I do it will all be worth it," he said as he patted his forehead with a hand-kerchief.

"Don't rush it," Isoline said. "Let me enjoy being the

center of attention for once before I'm locked away as the lady of the manor."

"You'll hardly be locked away," Geraldine, the wife of Isoline's eldest brother said as she entered the room. "You'll have more responsibility than you know what to do with as a baroness."

"Thankfully I will have Cyril's mother to help train me in all those matters," Isoline said.

Geraldine pressed her lips, but said nothing. Of course, they both knew the cliché of meddling obnoxious mothers-in-law, and many of their own friends suffered at the hands of an overbearing one, but Geraldine married into the family after Isoline's own mother had passed, so she had no experience in that area. Cyril's mother had so far seemed pleasant enough, but how she would be as a mother-in-law once Isoline moved into the family estate was anyone's guess. Isoline preferred to imagine she and the current Baroness Crowden would continue to get along after she and Cyril exchanged vows.

The rest of the day continued in much the same manner, with everyone rushed and harried in preparation for what should be the most important evening of Isoline's life. Of course, her actual marriage would be the crowning moment, but this was when everything would be made official: she would be named as the future Baroness Crowden —wife, heiress, Lady. Everything would change after tonight.

*T*he sun began to set before the guests started to arrive. Cyril and his parents were the first to arrive, as was proper. Isoline expected her heart to leap in excitement as he stepped out of the carriage, but she felt something else, something completely unexpected.

Dread.

As he climbed the stairs of the house to greet her, she felt the inexplicable urge to run. Run far and fast and never look back. She couldn't explain this sudden feeling of terror sitting deep within her stomach. She had known Cyril for years, long before he started courting her a couple of months before, and she had never felt anything akin to fear of him. Even if he had not courted her, he was someone within her sphere of acquaintances and could even be counted among her friends. This sudden sensation of fright was unsettling to her.

"My darling," he said as he bounded the steps and gripped her hands. His smile stretched from ear to ear. Indeed, he had always seemed more excited about the prospect of their marriage than she did. While she hoped to one day love him, she was certain he already loved her. He was kind, thoughtful, and considerate of her in all things. That she didn't appreciate him to the same extent filled her with shame. But what was she to do? She couldn't force herself to have feelings that simply did not exist. But she would do her best to be a loyal and dutiful wife to him. That was why she sent the man in her dreams away.

The man in her dreams.

Was he behind this? Was he causing her to have this irrational fear of Cyril? She had never noticed him having an effect on her during her waking hours before. Was such a thing even possible?

According to Descartes it was. At different points in her life, Isoline questioned the nature of her dreams, and even her own mind. She had sought an answer to what was happening to her. Descartes, the seventeenth-century French philosopher, had wondered if there was any difference between being awake and being in a dream. When we think we are awake, how do we know we are not in a dream, he had asked.

Isoline had posed the opposite question: when she was in a dream, how did she know she was not awake? Were her dreams simply an extension of her real life? Or were they perhaps another life? A life she was living at night not unlike the life she lived during the day, just separately.

Of course, she had not gone to school like her brothers. By the time she started having dreams and started researching philosophy, she was beyond the age of having a governess or tutor, not that her governess or tutor ever discussed such weighty matters with her anyway. And when she tried to talk about such things with her father, he simply patted her on the head and encouraged her to focus on her embroidery or to go for a ride. When her brothers were home, she tried to talk to them, but they had no interest in philosophy or the metaphysical world. Her eldest brother, Royston, studied politics, and her other brother, Laurence, was a man of science. And certainly, none of her female friends had any interest or understanding of the questions she posed. After a while, she put away her Descartes and simply had to accept the dreams as they were, with no explanation.

Until now.

As Cyril led her into the house by the hand, his touch turned into something like revulsion in her stomach. She could not wait for the first excuse to slip her hand from his grasp.

"I must see to the guests!" she said as she quickly excused herself. She flew to the butler, who was serving welcome drinks to the honored visitors and helped herself to one, two glasses of wine.

"I can do this," she muttered to herself. "I would be crazy not to go through with this." She fanned herself with her hand as she tried to calm her panicking heart.

"Isoline..."

She gasped as she felt his touch on her arm. Not his touch, but his hand just beyond her skin, just like she felt in her dream last night. She looked over her shoulder, but he was not there.

"Stop!" she whispered harshly as she ran to a small side room and shut the door. "Whoever you are, you must stop! I have a life to live. Leave me alone!"

But even as she said the words, she wanted to take them back. The idea of not having him in her life, even though she did not know him, filled her with sadness. She already felt a pain at the loss of him. It wasn't that she wanted him to go, it was that she wanted him to be real. If only she could somehow will him into existence.

"Isoline!" Her other sister-in-law, Eunice, grabbed her arm and pulled her into the main parlor, which had been cleared of furniture to make room for more socializing space and, later, dancing. "It is time for the toasts!"

As Isoline entered the room, a round of applause broke out.

"There she is!" he father said, wearing the biggest smile she had ever seen him don. It was unnatural on a face that usually looked at her sternly.

Cyril took her hand and brought it to his mouth, kissing

the back of it gently as he smiled. She tried to smile back, but she felt the edges of her mouth quiver.

Her father raised his glass. "I had only hoped to live long enough to see the last of my children finally settled," he said. "But to see my youngest child, my only daughter, married to such a fine young man as Cyril Hawtree, well, that is a blessing I could never have expected or even dreamed of."

Isoline's throat nearly closed up at the mention of the word dream. She felt she was going to be sick.

"To Isoline and Cyril!" her father said.

"To Isoline and Cyril!" everyone else chimed in as they raised their glasses and then took a sip. They all then turned to the presumably happy couple.

"And I could not be more honored to have such an amiable father-in-law," Cyril said. Everyone made an aww sound. "But to try to put into words how much I love and look forward to marrying this woman right here next to me..." He paused, and Isoline thought she saw him tearing up.

"Don't..." she started to say, but she did not know how to finish. Don't what? Don't cry? Don't say it? Don't marry me?

"When you have a title," he dared to say, "you grow up fearing that love will not play a role in your marriage. After all, when so many people depend on you, such important decisions cannot be made on flights of fancy. But when Isoline allowed me to court her, I knew that love would certainly play a part in my marriage."

Everyone gasped and murmured happy words. Some women even held their handkerchiefs to their eyes. But Isoline began to shake. She couldn't do this to him. She couldn't let him marry someone who didn't love him back.

He deserved better.

"To my future wife, and the love—"

"Stop," Isoline finally said, interrupting Cyril as he raised a glass to her. The room went silent. She looked around at the sea of faces. Her eyes fell on her father, the cold sternness returning to its usual place.

"What is it darling?" Cyril asked. "Do you wish to say something?"

Isoline looked him straight in the eyes. If she was going to cut out his heart, the least she could do was meet his gaze as she did it.

"I can't marry you."

CHAPTER TWO

*H*er father railed at her all night.

"How could you be so selfish? So ungrateful!" he yelled as she sat on the one chair the footmen had brought back into the parlor, her eyes downcast, her hands folded tightly in her lap.

"Yes, Papa," she said.

He paced like an angry beast about to strike. And truly, he was within his right to do so if he chose. After the guests filed out silently, no doubt saving their gossip for the safety of their enclosed carriages and parlors, surely none of them would begrudge her father for punishing her in the most corporal of manners.

"This is an absolute disgrace! The shame you have just brought on this family!"

"Yes, Papa," she agreed. She knew she could say no more. Even her brothers and their wives stood silently aside as her father stalked back and forth. They were undoubtedly disappointed in her as well. Her marriage to a baron would have increased the status of the entire family. While none of them would ever have titles, the marriage prospects for their own children would be much improved. Royston and Geraldine already had two sons of their own. Laurence and Eunice did not yet have children, but Isoline suspected that Eunice was with child and only waiting for her quickening to make the announcement. Eunice had put on weight and had not been able to eat meat lately without feeling ill. There had been many knowing glances shared across the dinner table between them, but nothing said officially. They would let Eunice make the announcement when she was ready.

She wished Eunice would speak up now, or any of them. She was always a disappointment to her father, but her brothers and their wives had always been among Isoline's closest friends. That they now, through their silence, indicated their approval of the way her father berated her stung more than the words her father spat at her.

But could she really expect them to come to her defense? After she told Cyril she could not marry him, she saw a handsome, confident, high-class man crumple in on himself.

"W-w-what are you saying?" he had stumbled to ask. "Do...do you wish to delay the date? I know it has been rushed, but I thought that was what you wanted..."

"I don't want to delay," she had said as gently as possible, though she doubted it was possible to gently crush someone's dreams. "I want to call it off altogether. I'm sorry."

His mouth opened and closed a few times like a fish. He simply had no words, and she did not expect him to. He finally handed his glass to the butler and left the house, dragging what little bit of his dignity he had with him.

The guests began to whisper and head for the door themselves, the celebration obviously at an end. Eunice and

Geraldine had done their best to salvage the situation, running to say goodbye to everyone and apologizing on behalf of their father-in-law, who obviously had no idea there was anything amiss with his confused daughter.

Why Isoline did what she did seemed of little importance to Vincent Beresford as he ranted and raved at her until the wee hours of the dawn. He never once asked her why, and, Isoline supposed, it truly didn't matter. The match was a good one, by any standard. That Cyril loved Isoline was only a bonus, a bonus any young woman in her position would be grateful to have.

"Oh, but not you," her father sneered. "Money, power, position, love. Your own family. What does any of it matter to you? You are a selfish, spoiled brat who doesn't deserve a roof over her head."

"Yes, Papa," she repeated so many times she lost count. But this one seemed to not have the desired effect.

"Don't you 'yes, Papa' me, damn girl," he snapped, ceasing his pacing and standing right in front of her. "I mean it! Someone like you has no place in this family or this house. I want you out!"

For the first time in hours, she raised her head and dared to look at him. "What...what can you mean?" she asked.

"Your wedding was to take place on the first of June," he said. "If you are not out of this house by then, I'll throw you out into the street myself."

"Papa!" she cried, jumping to her feet. "I'm sorry! I...I just couldn't..."

"Father!" Royston finally said, daring to take a step forward, speaking and moving for the first time in hours. "You can't do that. The scandal!"

"You think the scandal of disowning a disobedient and

disloyal child would be worse than the scandal she has already brought to this family?" her father asked. "Look, the sun is rising. Don't you think this is going to be in every society page between here and London as soon as the paper hits the stoop?"

"But a daughter on the street?" Geraldine asked. "That is much worse! At least her...her virtue is still intact! On the street, she'd be counted as a...a fallen woman."

"Yes!" Eunice pipped up hopefully. "As it is, we can just call it an indiscretion of youth. She can still marry someone else. If she ends up on the street, her chances of marrying will be over."

Isoline couldn't believe what the women were saying, even though she knew their words to be true. How could they talk about her virtue as if it were a family commodity!

"But I don't..." Isoline started to say, but then thought better of it. This was a family affair after all. What she wanted had no place in the discussion—even though it was her desires that had brought them to this low point.

"You...don't...what?" her father asked pointedly. No, he demanded to know.

Isoline gulped, trying to moisten her parched throat before answering. "I do not wish to marry anyone," she finally said.

If it had been possible, she thought she heard the entire county gasp in shock.

But it was true. She couldn't deny it. If she had learned anything over the last few hours it had been the clarity that until she either discovered the source of her dreams or found a way to end them, she did not want to marry. She couldn't. She'd had the opportunity to marry the best man available and she not only squandered that opportunity, she had hurt him dearly. She would never forgive herself for that. And she would never hurt another man like that again.

Her father had not been one to gasp. In fact, he didn't make a move while her brothers held their hands to their mouths in shock and Eunice had to be led to a chair by Geraldine lest she faint. But finally, he spoke.

"Two months," he said. "You have two months to leave this house of your own accord or I *will* throw you out." He then turned on his heels and headed for the parlor door.

"Father," Royston said, but he seemed unable to find any words to follow. Eunice and Geraldine burst into tears.

Isoline ran to her father and fell at his feet. "Papa!" she cried. "I'm so sorry. Please forgive me! I didn't mean for this to happen!"

Her heart calmed as he turned to her. Surely, he didn't mean what he said. He would forgive her. But as she looked up into his face, he saw that his resolve at been set in stone. He had always been stern, expecting nothing less than perfection from his children, but now she saw nothing but a cold detachment.

"Two months," he repeated. He left the room, sliding the parlor door closed behind him.

Dear Miss Beresford,

While we greatly appreciate your application, we have selected another candidate for the position. Good luck in your endeavors.

Sincerely,

Lady Montjoy

*I*t was the third rejection letter for a governess position Isoline had gotten in as many days. She crumpled the letter up and tossed it into the waste bin. She then buried her face in her hands and tried not to cry. She had cried so much over the previous weeks, though, she was very nearly out of tears to shed.

Her two months had dwindled down to two weeks. She had sent countless inquiries around the country offering her services as a governess, but none had responded favorably. She knew it had been a longshot. Even though she considered herself reasonably educated for a woman of her station, it was clearly not enough to recommend her as a teacher of other young ladies. She also feared her reputation may have traveled faster than her inquiries. Her father had been partially right about the society pages. While her abrupt dissolution of her engagement had happened too soon to make the papers that morning, it was certainly in all the papers in the county the next day. It was in the London papers the day after that. And it was in every paper in the country by the end of the week. No one would want a girl so flighty and irresponsible as she to be teaching manners and morals to their own daughters.

But the worst part was that the man had not visited her dreams once since that fateful night.

A couple of times, she had woken up in the glade. But she had been alone. Or at least she thought she was. She had no idea how she got there if he hadn't called her, but he did not respond when she called out. And she could not even sense his presence.

She had told him to leave her alone. To stop haunting her. Had he listened? Had he obeyed?

Had she made a terrible mistake?

She had not heard from Cyril since the night of the party, and she had not reached out to him. Geraldine and Eunice had taken the lead in returning the engagement gifts and sending notes of thanks on her behalf, but she herself had not spoken to anyone. While she had forced herself to send letters of inquiry for a position, she could not bring herself to face anyone she knew personally. She had not even been to church, which, of course, was another scandalous act she could add to her growing list, but one that was the least of her concerns. Paramount was having a place to live and food to eat when her deadline arrived.

More and more, as the days passed and the first of June drew closer, she considered going to see Cyril. Perhaps if she threw herself at his feet, begged his forgiveness, and rightfully accepted all blame, he would take her back. If the man in her dreams was gone, there was no reason she shouldn't marry Cyril. She could just plead cold feet. A foolish fear of change taken too far.

"I was waiting until after your wedding to announce that Lawrence and I are expecting," Eunice finally admitted to her over tea. "We are thrilled, but I didn't want to take away from your happy day. But I wonder if I should tell Father now, to help lighten his mood."

Eunice and Geraldine called their father-in-law simply "Father" as a sign of respect even though they both still had living papas of their own.

"I don't think anything would lighten his mood at this point," Isoline said sadly. "I've ruined everything. He will never forgive me."

Eunice reached over and took her hand. "Forever is a

long time," she said with a wan smile. "As is love. I'm sure there is nothing in the world my little one could do that would make me stop loving her."

"Her?" Isoline asked, the right side of her mouth quirking up.

"Father has two grandsons. Time for a granddaughter, don't you think?" she asked with a wink.

"You are far more kindly than Papa, though," Isoline said. "Unless..."

"Unless?" Eunice asked, raising her eyebrow.

Isoline placed her cup down, a sign she was about to say something serious. "Have you heard anything about Cyril? How he is...coping?"

Eunice pressed her lips and stared into her cup, clearly not wanting to say anything.

"Please, sister, tell me," Isoline pleaded.

"He's devastated, Isoline," Eunice said, her own eyes near to tears. "His sister told my cousin who told me that he is simply inconsolable. He only mopes around the house, even weeks later."

Isoline shook her head. She had not left her house for shame, not heartbreak. Surely, he could see the benefit of getting on with his life. Of fresh air, at least.

"Do you think, if I were to call, to apologize and please my case," Isoline said. "Do you think he would take me back?"

Eunice sighed and thought for a moment before responding. "I think that if it were only up to him, he might be willing to at least listen."

"But...?" Isoline prompted.

"But it isn't only up to him, is it?" she asked, shaking her head. "It never is with families, especially one like his. You insulted not just him, but the whole family. His mother, as kindly as she may have been to you before, is still furious. She'd never allow it. And even if she did, she'd never forgive you. She'd make every day of your life miserable until she died."

"It would be a penance equal to my crime," Isoline said. "I would deserve to be punished for the rest of my life if he took me back."

Eunice gripped Isoline's hand and shook her head. "No! Don't think that way. You...you just made a mistake. As we all do! You can't punish yourself forever over it. Something else will come along."

"I have only days left," Isoline said. "Father has not wavered in his resolve to toss me out if I'm not married or gone by his deadline. I'm out of options."

"*I*soline..."

Her eyes shot open. She grabbed her robe as she jumped out of bed. "I'm here," she said. "Though you would show up now. Now that I have decided to go back to Cyril and beg his forgiveness. How can you come back here now?"

She turned left and right in the darkness, but still she did not see him. But unlike her dreams of the past two months, she knew he was here.

"Show yourself," she said, as she had so many times before. "You have cost me everything! The least you can do is show me your face."

She could feel his breath on the back of her neck, but every time she tried to face him, she saw nothing.

She buried her face in her hand. "I'm crazy. I must be. Who would throw away her entire life for a man she's never seen? One who isn't even real!" She laughed and sobbed in equal measure. Now that he was here, that he had returned to her, she knew she couldn't ask Cyril for forgiveness. She couldn't be the wife he needed and deserved. But what was she going to do?

"I need your help," she finally said. "If you are listening to me, I need help. I am going to be disowned and banished in a matter of days."

She waited, but there was no response.

She wrapped her arms around herself and dropped her head. It was hopeless. This man had ruined her life and offered nothing in return.

What had she done?

She felt warm strong arms wrap around her from behind. She didn't move. She had a feeling that if she opened her eyes or tried to look at him, he would vanish. He held her tighter, and she relaxed into his comforting embrace.

"All will be well..."

In all the years the man had been visiting her, he had never said more than her name, and he had never touched her.

Her eyes opened wide and she lifted her head. "What?" she asked. She turned, and was back in her own bed.

*I*soline nervously tapped her foot as she sat at the dining table along with Eunice, Geraldine, Royston, and Lawrence. Their father had called a family meeting, the first such meeting since the night she called off her engagement, and it was the last day of May. Isoline had not called on Cyril, and she had received only more rejections to her governess inquiries. This would be the moment that decided her fate.

"He's forgiven you. Changed his mind," Eunice whispered from across the table. "I know he has."

"Then you don't know Father," Royston mumbled.

"He can't toss his own kin out on her ear," Eunice shot back. "Besides, why would he have called us all together unless he had changed his mind?"

"To explain what will happen tomorrow?" Geraldine surmised. "Tell us where Isoline will be taken and that we are never to speak to her again?"

"Shut your mouth," Eunice shot back.

"That's enough, Eunice," Lawrence said as he chewed nervously on what was left of his thumbnail.

"Look," Royston said, stepping up as the eldest sibling. "Whatever Father says, we will just nod along. Don't anger him, it will only make things worse. Just hear him out, then we will decide what to do."

Isoline's heart swelled at that. She hadn't spoken much to her brothers over the last couple of months. She knew they loved her, but she didn't want to cause problems between them and Papa, so she kept her distance. But they had often given her sympathetic glances, and she had spoken to her sisters-in-law. She knew the boys were simply playing it safe. Waiting to see what actually happened before speaking their piece. She felt in her heart that her brothers would not abandon her.

The door to the dining room opened and they all stood. Their father didn't say a word as he entered and took his seat, except to clear his throat to indicate they could all sit, which they did.

"Isoline," he said, addressing her directly for the first time in two months. "I know you sent inquires out about governess positions. Did you find a placement?"

"No, Papa," she said.

"And you have not reconciled with Cyril?" he asked, as if he did not know the answer. She would have told him if she had.

"No, Papa," she answered anyway.

"Very well," he said. "In that case, what happens to you now falls to me. I want you to know that I am still gravely disappointed by your actions, and what I do now does not lessen the severity of your indiscretion."

She felt her heart beat furiously in her chest at his words. He wasn't going to toss her out. He had changed his mind!

"Of course, Papa," she said.

"Very well," he said. He reached into his jacket and pulled a single piece of paper out. He slid it and a pen toward her.

It was a contract.

"The Dowager Countess of Payne, Bellamira Granville, does hereby employ the services of Miss Isoline Beresford as a companion for the foreseeable future at the stipend outline below..." Isoline read out loud. She then turned to her father. "What is this?"

"You remember your Grand-Aunt Bellamira?" he asked.

"I know *of* her," Isoline said. "But I've never met her."

"My God, is she even still alive?" Royston asked.

"Somehow, she is," their father said. "She just turned ninety. And she still lives in old Thornrush Manor on the coast. I wrote to her myself, on your behalf, Isoline, and offered your services as a companion. To my shock, she accepted."

Isoline was touched that it was her father who had found her a placement, even if he had been the reason she needed to find a placement in the first place. She wondered what he would have done if grand-auntie had turned the offer down, but she supposed it didn't matter now.

"Who is Grand-Aunt Bellamira?" Eunice asked.

"I'm not even sure how she is related to us anymore," Lawrence said.

"Great-great-great-great Aunt, ten times removed or something, I think," Royston helpfully explained. "She was married to the old Earl of Payne decades ago. He died before they had children, and there were no other male heirs at the time. The title left the family, went to some lucky bastard who was a friend of the king while she inherited the money and estate. But she never remarried or had children, so she just sits up there in the manor house with her money all alone. She's never named an heir. No idea what will happen to it all when she finally kicks it."

"With any luck," their father spoke up, "it will go to Isoline."

Geraldine gasped. "Surely, she didn't make Isoline her heiress?"

"Not yet," he said. "But with Isoline there as her companion, if she pleases the old bat, who knows?"

"Wait." Isoline finally dared to speak up. "You want me to be a companion to grand-auntie with the hopes that she will name me her heir?"

"Yes," her father replied simply. "If you refuse to help the family by marrying well, then you can still be of service by inheriting well."

"I can't force her to make me her heir," Isoline said. "What if she doesn't choose me?"

"At least you won't be any worse off than you are now," her father said with a clear hint of warning.

Isoline needed to come home an heiress, or not come home at all.

CHAPTER THREE

"*All will be well...*"

How did he know? Isoline pondered the man's words as the carriage rumbled along. She lazily looked out the window at the encroaching sea. She had never been to the coast before. She had always imagined it would be bright with sunshine and fresh air, but she was wrong. It was the beginning of summer, in the middle of the day, and the sky was dark and grey as a winter evening. It was not as cold as winter, but the black clouds and wet air gave her a chill that had her clutching her wrap to her throat.

While the mysterious man's words should have been a comfort to her—they did come to pass, after all—she wondered just how much he knew. How could he have known that her father was making arrangements with Grand-Aunt Bellamira? She would have to ask him, though she had no idea if he would reply. She had been asking him questions for years, but he had never responded. She shook her head as she thought about just how much faith she had put into this man who walked in her dreams. Even if she hadn't called off her wedding, she had delayed courtship for years because of him. She had been a foolish girl, but was she much better as an adult? She had not thrown herself at the feet of Cyril as she should have the moment the man returned to her dreams. How many more decisions would she make based on a fantasy? She hoped none, but she knew better.

It began to rain.

She leaned over to look out the window, and the clouds that had only been a gentle covering before had bellowed into a frightening summer storm.

"Should we stop somewhere?" Isoline called out to the driver. The lanterns strapped to the side weaved about wildly. She wondered how they stayed attached.

"Nah, miss," he said. "A bit of rain never hurt no one. Hai-yah!" He whipped the horses, sending them into an even faster gallop, tossing her back in her seat.

She pulled herself back upright and looked out the window at the road ahead. She gulped when she saw that it narrowed and hugged the upcoming cliff edge. She wiped a few raindrops from her brow. She pulled the curtains closed and tied them tightly shut. The driver might feel confident, but she did not, and she certainly did not have to watch while he faced down the dangers of the road. Unfortunately, with the heavy curtains drawn, the inside of the carriage was nearly pitch black. There was nothing she could do except sit back and feel every bump and jolt.

"Whoa! Look out!" the driver called, and Isoline was pitched from her seat to the floor. Thankfully, the seats were cushioned, so she did not injure herself greatly, but she could not help but scream for fright.

She heard the horses whinny and the driver yell as she felt the carriage start to tip onto its side. She felt herself thrown into the air and scrambled for something, anything to grip onto. She finally grabbed the edges of the window as the carriage crashed to the ground. Her fingers slipped from the wet windowpane and she fell hard against the other door.

"H-help!" she called out, but she could hear nothing over the panicked whinnying of the horses. "Driver? Are you there?"

She got to her feet, but she could not reach other door to open it. It was now too far above her. The window covering had come partially undone, so she could see the dark sky above, but not much else. A few drops of rain fell on her face, but it was not raining heavily, only drizzling. She felt as though she were in a dark, wet pit.

She sighed in annoyance. There was nothing she could do but wait. The driver must have been injured in the fall. Surely, someone would come along eventually and help her out. She started to feel around for a blanket or pillows she could use to sit on to make her wait more comfortable when a distinctly unpleasant smell wafted past her nose.

Smoke!

She listened and heard a crackling and realized the smoke was filling the carriage.

"Help! Help me!" she screamed as she realized that the carriage lanterns must have caught the wreckage on fire. The horses cried, and she could feel the carriage shake. They must have still been attached to it and were trying to escape.

The smoke filled her nose and burned her eyes. She jumped up and down, trying to grab the door above her, but it was always beyond her reach.

"Please! For the love of God!" she yelled. She knew no one was there, no one to hear her pleas, but in the moment, there was nothing else she could do. She was going to die on an abandoned road in a fire in the rain. What an uncere-monious end to a pathetic life not yet lived.

The carriage started to grow hot and the smoke filled her lungs. She coughed and leaned against the wall of the carriage, waiting to pass out. But then, she heard a snap, and blue light filled the carriage. She looked up and saw a hooded man standing over her. He had opened the door and was now leaning inside, holding his hand out to her. She did not say anything, she only jumped and grabbed his hand. With uncanny strength, he pulled her from the wreckage. He held her tightly in his arms and leaped down, carrying her a safe distance away. He deposited her under a tree, which shielded her somewhat from the rain.

"The horses," she mumbled, her voice gravely. "And the driver! He's hurt!"

The man nodded and ran back toward the carriage. Only then did she realize the extent of the danger she was in. The carriage was nearly engulfed in flames. Surely, she would have been dead very soon had she not been rescued at that moment. One horse was on the ground, most certainly dead. She could not see the driver, but the other horse was in a complete panic, rearing up on his hind legs and kicking his front ones in complete terror. She saw the man draw a knife and attempt to cut the poor beast loose.

Her eyes burned from the smoke and exhaustion. She closed them and let the tears come, partly from fear, partly from relief, and partly to allow the tears to clear the smoke and ash.

"My dear, are you all right?" a voice asked her.

She looked up as the man kneeled down by her and pulled down his hood. She could only shake her head.

"Was there anyone else in the carriage?" he asked.

"N-no," she managed to say. "Only myself, and the driver."

"I fear the driver is dead," he said sympathetically. "As is one of the horses. The other one took off like the devil himself was on his tail. I doubt we will see the poor creature again. Thank goodness I happened by! Here." He wrapped a blanket around her.

"Th-th-thank you," she managed to say. "What happened?"

"I was going to ask you the same thing," he said. "But these roads can be treacherous."

She nodded. A freak accident.

"Where were you headed?" he asked. "Not many people live in these parts."

"Thornrush Manor," she said. "To see my grand-aunt."

"Your aunt?" he asked with happy surprise. "Lady Bellamira is a grand-aunt of mine as well! We must be cousins! Well, quite distant ones anyway." He gave her a smile and squeezed her arm.

She chanced a look at his face. Distant, indeed. He must have been from a completely different branch of the family because she was sure she had not seen him before. He looked to be in his late twenties with fair hair and eyes so green she could see the color even in the dark light of the stormy sky. She tried to give him a smile in return, but felt exhausted and cold. She shivered.

"Dear cousin, are you injured?" he asked.

She shook her head.

"Then let me help you," he said. "My own horse is here. I can take you to Thornrush myself."

The idea of moving from the safe spot on the ground sent her heart to racing, but she knew she could not stay here forever. She gave a small nod. He leaped up and was back in barely a moment with his own brown horse. He took her hand and helped her to her feet. He then climbed up on his horse and pulled her up in front of him. She sat sideways and snuggled into his chest. He kept a protective arm around her as he started the horse into a slow trot.

"By the way, cousin, I didn't get your name," he said.

"Isoline," she said as she felt herself start to relax.

"I'm Tristan," he replied.

*I*soline wondered if she had fallen asleep because it seemed like she had only blinked her eyes and they were trotting up to the largest manor house she had ever seen.

The house looked nearly cobbled together from many other smaller ones. Windows of every shape and size lined the front, and spires reached up into the dark sky. As they approached the front of the house, the door seemed to open automatically and a well-starched butler stood by.

Tristan leaped down from the horse with ease and then helped Isoline to her feet. He reached down as though to carry her, but she gently pushed him away.

"I think I can walk," she said. "I'm much better now, thank you."

In truth, she was stiff and her head still swimming from the ordeal, but she could not suffer the indignity of being carried inside to her meet her aunt for the first time.

Tristan nodded and held onto her arm protectively nonetheless, and she did not refuse his aid.

"Talbot," Tristan addressed the butler. "There was a terrible accident on the road and Miss Beresford's carriage toppled. All of her luggage was left behind, if it survived. Can you send someone to fetch what is left? And arrangements will need to be made for the driver. He didn't make it."

Talbot nodded. "I will take care of it," he said in a short but not curt manner.

Tristan led her inside, and she could not help but gasp at the grandeur of the inside of the house. It donned on Isoline then that it was truly what only the wealthiest of people considered to be a "comfortable" country house. Before her was a large staircase lined with red carpeting. Up above, the gallerys for the second and third floors could be seen. She turned in a slow circle as she tried to take in every aspect of the imposing foyer. A crystal chandelier larger than a person hung above her. On the walls, the faces of former occupants of the house were framed in gilt. Two Ming vases stood on either side of the base of the staircase.

"Don't just stand there dripping," a voice called down to her.

Isoline looked up and saw a woman standing at the top of the staircase. Isoline was sure she had not been standing there before. She must have appeared while Isoline was busy gawking.

The woman gingerly lifted the edge of her gown as she carefully descended the stairs.

"You wouldn't believe the cost to have a rug of this size cleaned," the woman said as she approached.

"Now, Aunt Bellamira," Tristan chided. "Isoline has had quite a fright. Be kind."

The woman stood in front of Isoline and clasped her long thin fingers together in front of her.

Isoline couldn't help but stare at the woman in surprise. This was her ninety-year-old, great, great, great, great, too-many-greats-to-count Grand-Auntie Bellamira Granville, the Dowager Countess of Payne? The woman had grey hair, but that was the only indication of her age. She didn't look a day over fifty, in Isoline's estimation. Her eyes were clear and bright blue. Her face was surprisingly smooth, with only a few lines around her eyes and mouth. She was thin and stood ramrod straight. The deep purple of her old-fashioned gown brought a healthy color to her cheeks.

"A fright?" Bellamira asked. "Of what sort?"

"The carriage," Isoline explained. "It crashed and burned. The driver was killed. I was so fortunate that Tristan happened by when he did." She looked up at him affectionately and he smiled back with a gentle squeeze of her arm she realized he was still holding.

Bellamira pressed her lips, her only reaction to the harrowing tale of Isoline's near-death experience.

"I still don't see what that has to do with ruining a perfectly fine rug," Bellamira said with an exasperated sigh but the edge of one side of her mouth turned up. Isoline thought this was her aunt's way of making a joke, but she wasn't sure. "Come this way."

Bellamira walked them through two other large rooms, each furnished with tables, chairs, and paintings, before opening the door to a parlor room. There were two couches sitting opposite each other next to a roaring fire in an elegant fireplace.

"Please sit," Bellamira said, motioning to one of the couches. She sat first, and then Isoline sat across from her. Once he was sure she was settled, Tristan released her arm and sat on the couch next to Bellamira.

Isoline didn't realize just how chilled she had been until

the warmth of the fire wafted over her. She sighed and held her hands to it.

"Oh, thank you," she said. "This is just what I need. My nerves are so taut."

The door to the parlor opened and Talbot came in with a tea tray complete with biscuits. Isoline's mouth started to water instantly. Talbot prepared her a cup of tea with cream and two sugars and placed a biscuit on the saucer as he handed her the cup.

"Talbot, you seem to have read my mind," Isoline said as she accepted the tea eagerly. She sipped the tea and then ate the biscuit in nearly one bite, she was so famished. "Please, forgive my manners. I have no idea how long it has been since I have eaten."

"Not at all," Bellamira said. "It is only natural after your experience. Talbot, what is the current situation?"

Bellamira must run her house like clockwork, Isoline thought. She had only just heard about Isoline's accident herself, yet she knew that Talbot would already have a handle on the situation. If nothing else, Isoline knew she would learn a thing or two about running a house from her aunt.

"I sent James to fetch the lady's things, if there is anything to salvage," Talbot explained. "Marcus has been sent to town to alert the vicar and the constable regarding the driver."

"Very good," Bellamira said as she accepted her own teacup. Talbot then handed a cup to Tristan before retreating to the edge of the room to await any further instructions.

"So," Bellamira said, "other than the dramatic end, how was the rest of your journey? It was quite far, I think."

"Indeed," Isoline said as she placed her cup on the

saucer. "I was able to take a train to York, but then had to hire a carriage to bring me here. The driver came highly recommended. I can't imagine what happened..." The crash began to replay in her mind and she shuddered. She shook her head to try and push the images away.

"Men can be fools, reckless," Bellamira said, then she glanced at Tristan. "Present company excluded, of course."

"You are too kind, auntie," he said, and the two shared a laugh. Isoline smiled but was still too out of sorts to find humor in the situation.

"Grand-Auntie," Isoline said, hoping to change the subject. "Tristan believes we may be related in some way. Would you know how?" She held her teacup up for seconds and hoped Talbot would include a few more biscuits as well. He did not disappoint.

Bellamira waved the question off. "Oh, one brother had a mess of daughters and a brother-in-law had a few of his own. They all married and left and had children of their own. At my age, who can keep track? If I even considered sending them all cards for Christmas I would have to start at New Year's."

"Maybe we should hire a genealogist," Tristan suggested. "Surely, as the family's matriarch you would want to see just how large the tree has gotten."

"Matriarch, am I?" Bellamira asked, mock surprise on her face. "I can't remember the last time a family member wrote to me for advice, or just to check on me. The only letters I receive are requests for help and money."

Isoline squirmed a bit. She thought Bellamira must be including her father in that stack of letters. Though she realized she was guilty of ignoring her grand-auntie.

"In fact, the last time I received something from a family member who did not ask for something in return was from

Isoline," Bellamira said, and Isoline nearly choked on her tea in shock. She couldn't remember what Bellamira was referring to.

"Oh, surely not," Isoline said. But Bellamira was insistent.

"It's true!" she said. "You had just turned fifteen and you sent me a portrait. I even have the letter that came with it." She stood and crossed the room. She opened a few drawers in a large chest and rummaged through them until she found what she was looking for and pulled it out. "Here. Not much, but I still remember it."

She handed the note to Isoline who read it eagerly.

Dear Grand-Aunt Bellamira,

I hope this letter finds you well. I am so sad we have never met, but I think of you often. In honor of my fifteenth birthday, my father commissioned a painting. I wanted you to have one so you may keep me in your thoughts and prayers as I do you.

Sincerely, your devoted niece,

Isoline Beresford

Isoline gave her aunt a smile. "Of course," she said. "How could I ever forget." As she read the note, she realized that she had not forgotten, but that it had never happened. The paintings did, she remembered keenly having to sit for them for hours. They had been completed only weeks before her mother died. But she had not sent one herself to her grand-aunt. Nor had she sent the note. But she knew who did. She instantly recognized her mother's handwriting. Her mother must have taken one of the paintings and sent it along with the note on her behalf. But she had no idea why. If her mother wanted to send a painting and note to her aunt, why did she not instruct Isoline to send the note herself. She would have done so even if she didn't understand her mother's motives. She was not one to argue with her mother overmuch.

Bellamira took the note back and held it in her hands as she sat back across from Isoline. "As you can see, Isoline, I don't *need* a companion." Isoline could not help but agree. If Bellamira truly was as old as she had been led to the believe, the woman did not show it. She seemed as healthy —physically and mentally—as a woman half her age. "But I suppose at my age I can understand why the extended family might think I need to have someone around. And if it had to be anyone, I suppose I am glad they chose you."

Isoline blushed. She wasn't sure why her mother did what she did, but it certainly paid off in the end. Isoline was a woman in need, and Bellamira, however begrudgingly, had been there for her, and Isoline was grateful.

"You are far too kind, auntie," Isoline said.

"Well, enough of this sentimentality," Bellamira said as she stood, followed by Isoline and Tristan. "It is far too late to have male visitors."

"I'll take that as my cue to leave," Tristan said with a smile. He gave a short bow to Bellamira, and then to Isoline. "I am truly glad I happened upon you, cousin. If you ever need anything, do not hesitate to ask."

"Thank you," was all Isoline managed to get out. She couldn't quite manage to bring herself to call this man her cousin, not yet.

As Tristan exited the parlor, a woman in a simple black dress who appeared to be in her mid-thirties entered the room.

"Miss Beresford's room is ready, my lady," she announced.

"Very good," Bellamira said. "Bess will be your maid,"

she told Isoline as they also left the parlor and started up the large staircase. "She will be waiting in your room. I know you lost your trunks and such for now, but Bess should have been able to find you something suitable to sleep in. When James returns we shall try to salvage your clothes, and if not, we can send for something from the village."

Isoline was nearly panting with exertion as they reached the top of the stairs, but Bellamira did not seem phased in the slightest.

"I am amazed at such efficiency," Isoline said. "I would imagine running a house such as this would be so complicated."

"Well, I have had many decades of practice," Bellamira said.

"Have you?" Isoline couldn't help but ask, even though as soon as she said it she realized how rude it must have sounded. Bellamira raised an eyebrow and looked at her. "I mean...excuse me, grand-auntie, but you look exquisite. I never would have guessed you are as old as everyone tells me."

"Everyone talks about my age, do they?" she asked as she turned and walked down the gallery. Isoline felt her face go hot with embarrassment, but then she realized Bellamira was once again attempting a joke. "Well, I can't really blame them, I suppose. It must be shocking to know I have outlived so many other much younger members of the family."

"Tristan wasn't kidding when he said you were the family matriarch," Isoline said, counting the doors as they passed, sure she would never find her room again.

"Clean living, no stress, and the grace of God," Bellamira said. "Those are the keys to a long, healthy life."

"You make it sound so simple," Isoline said.

"I know it is anything but," Bellamira said as she finally stopped in front of a door and opened it. A young woman inside the room gave a curtsey.

Isoline took her aunt's hand in her own and started for a moment at how cold it was. Bellamira seemed surprised by the gesture, but Isoline gave the hand a squeeze. "Thank you so much, grand-auntie, for everything."

Bellamira gave Isoline a small, uncomfortable smile, as if she were not used to the sensation, and slipped her hand away, turning Isoline toward the room. "Sleep well, my dear." She closed the door behind her.

"Can I help you undress, miss?" Bess asked. Isoline nodded and let Bess remove her dress and place her shoes in the hallway, most likely to be cleaned by a footman. Bess looked to be about Isoline's age, but she had copper red hair and freckles. Isoline had hoped to speak with Bess a bit and inspect her room before falling asleep, but as soon as her head landed on the fluffy pillow and Bess pulled the heavy down comforter over her, she was fast asleep.

She slept so deeply, she couldn't be bothered to dream.

CHAPTER FOUR

The next morning, Isoline was awoken by a gentle knock on her door.

"Miss Beresford," Bess called.

Isoline forced her eyes to open. The room was already bright with morning sunlight. "Yes, Bess," she said groggily. "Come in."

Bess entered the room and walked over to the window, throwing the curtain open brightly. "Did you sleep well, miss?" she asked. She didn't wait for an answer before she was stoking the fire and opening the door to the wardrobe to find Isoline something acceptable to wear.

"I think I passed right out," Isoline said as she squinted in the light and stretched her arm. "This is the most comfortable bed."

"Her ladyship has only the best of everything," Bess said as she laid out a terribly old-fashioned green dress. "James brought your cases in, miss," she explained. "But they were soaked through and quite a few things smelled of smoke. Jenny, she's our washerwoman, is going to salvage what she can after a brisk wash and dry, but that will take all day. Mr.

Talbot himself is going through your personal items, books and papers and such, and laying those out to dry as well. I hope you don't mind."

Isoline climbed out of bed and shook her head. "I don't mind. I don't think I have anything too scandalous among my thing, except possibly my books on dream theory," she said.

Bess prepared the bowl of wash water and helped Isoline remove her sleeping gown. "Dream theory, miss?"

"Have you ever wondered if your dreams have a deeper meaning?" Isoline asked. "Like, if you dream of falling, it could mean you feel as though your life is out of control."

"I think I would know that without a dream telling me," Bess said. "Do you often dream of falling? Sounds a bit frightening."

"Not exactly," Isoline said. "I just have very...realistic dreams, I suppose. As though I'm not dreaming at all but am quite awake."

"You poor thing," Bess said. "Sounds right exhausting." She helped Isoline towel off and then they got to work putting Isoline into her many layers of clothes. Isoline was surprised by how free-flowing the borrowed dress felt. It cinched up under her bosom, but the rest of the gown was light and billowy. It was nothing like the tight corset and full petticoats she normally wore. She felt almost indecent.

"Are you sure this is quite all right to wear?" Isoline asked as she looked at herself in the full-length mirror.

Bess couldn't suppress her smile. "You look lovely, miss," she said. "I think you'd look beautiful in whatever you wear."

"I'm not worried about that," Isoline said, turning to look at herself from the back. "I just think I might send the men into apoplexy if they see me in such a state. How did the ladies get away with such clothes back then?"

"I'm sure the menfolk won't mind a bit," Bess said with a chuckle. "And I doubt they will say anything. Lady Granville herself gave the approval for you to wear the things in this closet. They won't want to upset her by saying anything untoward."

Isoline nodded. "Of course. Thank you, Bess."

Bess gave a curtsey. "Lady Granville takes her breakfast in her room. But Mrs. Lawson, the cook, has had a breakfast tray sent for you to the dining hall."

"I'll be down shortly, then. Thank you, Bess."

Isoline took one last look at herself in the mirror and shook her head. Well, there was nothing she could do about the dress now. She had nothing else to wear for at least the day. She wandered over to the window to check the weather. She wondered if she would need only a light wrap or something heavier. As she looked out, she thought she saw someone duck behind a tree. She watched for a moment, but he never appeared from the other side. She shrugged. Aunt Bellamira had a full staff, she certainly had gardeners as well.

She opened the window and put her hand out. The clouds had cleared away from the day before so the weather was warmer and drier, but it was still surprisingly chilly for summer. She would have to get used to this northern weather. She thought a heavier wrap might be in order.

She went down to the dining room and was surprised to see a footman waiting to serve her tea with her breakfast.

"It makes me feel a bit out of sorts to have so many people waiting on me," she said with an uncomfortable chuckle. "Back home we had a much larger family but so few servants."

"I'm sure you will soon get used to the way things are run here, miss," he said with a smile.

"Of course..." she said.

"James, miss," he told her.

"Oh, James," she said as he handed her a cup of tea. "You are the one who fetched my bags last night, weren't you?"

"I was, miss," he said as he moved back to stand by the tea tray.

"That was so kind of you," she said. "I feel terrible that you were sent out in the rain so late."

"Not at all, miss," he said. "We are all just glad that you arrived safely."

Isoline started to relax a little as she enjoyed her breakfast. She thought that it would be awkward having so many servants around. She worried they might think that she was beneath their dignity to serve. She was of no importance, after all. Nothing like the Dowager Duchess of Payne. Isoline might be a distant relative, but her family carried no title and did not have much money. In fact, since her father had more or less disowned her, she was basically a poor relation in need of her grand-aunt's charity. But there was nothing but politeness and respect in the tone and actions of the staff. If anything, she felt well-cared for by them all, as though they thought she was a lost puppy in need of their coddling.

"I suppose I should call on my aunt now," she told James when she finished her meal.

"Her ladyship usually stays in her rooms during the morning," James explained. "She has breakfast and then reads or works on her correspondence. She doesn't tend to socialize with anyone except her maid until she comes down for luncheon. I believe your mornings will belong to you as well, miss."

"Oh," she said, a little disappointed. She was being given free room and board in exchange for being Bellamira's companion. It felt strange that she was not being called on to...companion. What exactly would Bellamira expect of her anyway? She supposed they would have to discuss her duties at luncheon.

"I think I will explore the house and grounds a bit then," she said. "I will need to learn my way around eventually."

"Of course, miss," James said as he walked over to the wall and showed her a dangling cord. "Most rooms have a cord like this. If you need anything, just pull it and someone will be along shortly. Though..." He paused.

"What is it?" she asked.

"I just realized that many of the rooms and cords haven't been used in many years. Some could be in disrepair. If they don't work, I think you could just stand out in the gallery and yell. Someone will be sure to hear you."

Isoline laughed, and James couldn't suppress a smile even though he was trying. "If I get scolded for screaming from the gallery I'll be sure to let them know that James had given me permission."

He smiled as he opened the door for her to leave the dining room. As she walked back to the main staircase, she was surprised that the house already felt less imposing than before. She nearly skipped up the staircase to the first-floor gallery. She realized that for the first time in months, she felt happy. Even when she had been engaged to Cyril, she was anxious about her future, concerned about marrying a man she didn't love. Would they be happy? Would they grow to hate each other? What did she know about marrying into the nobility? Would her mother-in-law be as kindly toward her after the wedding? How long would it be before she became a mother? What did she know of raising children? After she called off the engagement and her father announced his plans to disown her, she had been even more miserable and was then terrified of the future.

Now, she still did not know what the future held. How long would she stay? What if Bellamira died and didn't make her an heiress. What if she died and Bellamira *did* leave her an inheritance? Would her dreams ever go away? Would she ever marry? Would she end up an old spinster like her aunt? But all of those questions, while important, did not seem pressing. For the moment, she was taken care of and happy. What was it Bellamira said about the secrets to a long, healthy life? One of her tips had been no stress. As she breathed in deeply, she could certainly imagine that a life without cares or worries would contribute to a healthy and optimistic outlook.

She headed down the hallway opposite the direction to her bedroom to start her exploration. She started to open the first door, but then she realized that she didn't know which room was Bellamira's, and she didn't want to walk in unannounced, so she knocked. After a moment, she didn't hear anything, so she carefully turned the knob.

The door was locked.

She pouted in disappointment. The next door was also locked, as was the next. She couldn't imagine why the doors were all locked, but then, she didn't see a reason why they would be unlocked either. The rooms were unoccupied, so maybe having them locked meant they knew the rooms were at least left neat a tidy, even if they did get a bit dusty. The housekeeper probably had a schedule of which rooms to dust when and kept the doors locked the rest of the time. It made sense, but didn't leave much for Isoline to explore.

She wondered if the housekeeper would be willing to loan her a key.

At least the hallways themselves were somewhat interesting. Artwork seemed to hang on every available space, and not just paintings of old relatives. There were landscapes and still life, classic works in the Greek and Roman style, and even a scroll in an oriental style. Someone in the Granville family certainly had an appreciation for art. Isoline made a note to ask her grand-aunt about it when they spoke.

With exploring the house not an option, Isoline decided to explore the grounds instead. As she exited the front door, she was pleased to find that the temperature had increased from when she had tested the air that morning. She took a deep breath and enjoyed the fresh smell of the countryside. As she stood on the porch, she surveyed the land before her. Indeed, there was nothing else to look at but land. There was not another house or even a steeple to be seen. She knew there was a village somewhere nearby, but it was probably too far away to walk to.

She knew the grounds were expansive—they would have to be to support such a large house—but she had no idea just how large they were or what was to be found thereupon. But what was the fun of exploring if you knew exactly what you were going to find? She set out walking with no particular destination in mind. She assumed it would be easy enough to find her way back to the main house.

The stables were not very far from the house, and the grooms gave her a polite nod when she entered. By now, all of the staff for the entire estate must have known that Bellamira's niece had arrived. One of the grooms asked her if she would like him to saddle a horse for her. She told him no, that she was happy to explore on foot for now, but she was glad to know this would be an option in the future. She did enjoy riding. But for now, she was excited to be in the middle of nowhere and was looking forward to being alone for a few minutes.

She was surprised to see that she wasn't nearly as alone on the giant estate as she would have thought. Every so often, she would come across a man or a small group of men working the fields or with animals. After she left the barn, she came across sheep and pigs and the men tending them. Even when she came across a stream, a man in wading pants was fishing and some women were washing clothes.

She kept walking, hoping to find a bit of solitude eventually. After a long while, she stopped running across people. She crested a small hill and looked in every direction. She could not see the house. She suddenly realized that in her quest to be rid of people, she had also become completely lost. She was exhausted.

"Idiot," she chided herself. She sighed and plopped down on the ground to catch her breath and let her feet rest. She thought about James's recommendation to simply holler if she needed anyone, but she didn't think anyone would hear her out here. And if they did she would certainly look crazy for yelling. She wasn't quite desperate yet, though, so she took a moment to enjoy the view and the quiet.

The view was certainly stunning. She had never been in such a rural area before, and the gently rolling hills and bright greens of summer filled her with peace and happiness. She thought that she could live here for the rest of her life and be perfectly happy.

"Beautiful," a voice behind her said.

She started and looked up. A man was standing behind her. Her breath hitched in her throat. His hair and eyes were dark and he had a sun-kissed bronze to his skin. He was wearing a white shirt that was slightly open at the chest with the sleeves rolled up and black pants. He was one of the most handsome men she had ever seen and had to tear her gaze away to keep from staring.

"Yes," she finally said. "It is. I've never been in such a place."

"You are Isoline, Miss Beresford?" he said more than asked in a delicate, lilting accent she couldn't place. "Her ladyship's niece."

"I am," Isoline said as she stood. "I just arrived last night."

"I heard," he said. Isoline saw he was smiling. And not just politely, but a large smile as though he were the happiest man in the world. His smile was infectious and she could not suppress her own. She looked down and tucked her hair behind her ear.

"Yes, I suppose everyone has heard by now," she said.

"Very nearly," he said with a laugh. "At least everyone on the estate. But I'm sure the word will spread through the village today."

"You live on the estate?" she asked.

He nodded. "Yes, I rent a small cottage over that way." He pointed in a direction, but Isoline was quite turned around and could not tell if he was pointing north, south, east, or west or somewhere in between, but she nodded as though she understood.

It then dawned on her that she had no idea where she was and was completely alone with a strange man.

"I...I should head back," she said. "My aunt will send someone to look for me very soon."

"Of course," he said. "Don't let me keep you. I just saw you here and wanted to introduce myself."

"But you didn't," she said.

"Didn't what?" he asked.

"Introduce yourself," she said. "You haven't told me your name."

He closed his eyes and shook his head in embarrassment. "Forgive me," he said. "I am Auberon. Auberon Drochia."

"Drochia?" Isoline asked. "What an interesting name."

He nodded. "From the old country," he said. She assumed he meant one of the old countries on the continent, but he didn't indicate which one. "But we have lived here for many years."

"Here?" she asked, raising an eyebrow. "In England or on this estate?"

"Perhaps both," he said, and they both laughed.

Isoline was feeling easy and comfortable in Auberon's company, which told her she needed to excuse herself, more firmly this time. She wasn't lying when she had told her father she had no desire to marry. She didn't want to ever lead a man into heartache again.

She moved to leave. "I really must be going," she said. "But it was very nice to meet you."

"And you, dear Isoline," he said.

The way her name fell from his lips was like music to her ears. She longed to ask him to walk with her, so talk to him more and stay by his side for as long as possible, but she couldn't. She shouldn't. She started to walk down the hill but remembered she didn't know the way back to the house. She paused and looked both this way and that.

"The manor house is that way," Auberon said, pointing in one direction.

She blushed and nodded her thanks. "Of course," she said as though she had known all along.

As she walked down the hill and back toward the house, she was sure she could still feel his eyes on her long after she had left his sight.

CHAPTER FIVE

"*I*soline..."

That night, the man returned to her dream, and it was as though there had not been months of separation between them. She awoke, grabbed her robe, and stepped onto the wet grass. As she walked through the glen, she let her fingers caress the tips of the grass.

She knew he was there. She could sense him before he even approached. She stood still and let him get closer. She could feel his hand on her shoulder, hovering just beyond her skin. She broke out into gooseflesh and slightly shivered. From the corner of her eye, she could see his breath crystallizing in the night air. He was so close, yet she knew if she dared to try and look at him, he would vanish, and she wanted him to stay here with her.

"Thank you," she said. "You told me that all would be well, and it has been. I don't know if you played a part in it or if you just knew what my father and aunt were planning, but I am glad I didn't return to Cyril or find a governess position. I am happy here."

She heard him sigh in relief, and she felt his hand lay

slightly on her shoulder. She teared up for happiness, but she dared not move for fear it would break the spell. They stood there together for an indeterminable amount of time —Isoline had never been able to decipher if time passed differently in her dreams—until the dream finally faded and she woke back in her own bed. She felt completely rested and at peace.

" *I*'ve had a note from Tristan," her aunt announced as they ate luncheon together. At exactly noon, Aunt Bellamira had left her apartments and come downstairs where Isoline had been eagerly awaiting her. After her brisk walk the day before, she had returned filthy and exhausted and had proven to be poor company for her aunt for the afternoon and feel asleep early. Today, she intended to make up for it. She read quietly until Bellamira came downstairs and she was polite and attentive to every word the woman said, which wasn't much while they ate, the mention of Tristan being the first thing of note she said.

"Oh?" Isoline asked as she sipped her broth, the first course of the meal. "Did he say anything interesting?"

"Not in the least," Bellamira said as she waved the broth away and a pigeon compote was served along with some vegetables and bread. The food at Thornrush was something that Isoline was going to have to get used to. She was being served a large variety of food she had not eaten before and in such a quantity she was easily stuffed long before the dessert arrived. "Though he rarely does," she continued.

"Are you not fond of Tristan?" Isoline asked.

"Fond?" Bellamira asked as though it was a ridiculous question. "Well, I suppose he is pleasant enough, but he calls so often I nearly think he lives here. He never sends a note, though. Just drops by unannounced. I rather think the advanced warning was more for your benefit than mine."

"Mine?" Isoline asked, suddenly alarmed. "Why should he alert me to his visit?"

"He probably assumes you will want to be able to prepare yourself for his visit," Bellamira said as she picked at her luncheon. "Most ladies go to such extremes in preparing their faces and hair for a gentleman caller." Isoline noticed that her aunt never ate much of the exquisite food the cook prepared, which probably explained why she was so thin. Isoline tried to imitate her aunt's peckish nature, but the food was so delicious she didn't want a single morsel to remain on her plate.

Her face went hot at her aunt's words. She had hoped that by coming to Thornrush she would be well away from any possible suitors. She hadn't thought that she would have to start rebuffing advances from the very first man she met, the one who had saved her life! How could she turn him down when he was—by definition—her savior?

"Well, he has seen me at my worst already," Isoline said, her own appetite suddenly gone. "I sure I looked quite a fright, rain-drenched and travel-worn. I'm surprised I didn't frighten him off." She chuckled even though she found the situation anything but funny.

"Is that what you want?" Bellamira asked, signaling for the dishes to be taken away and a dessert of burnt cream brought out.

"Not...exactly..." Isoline said, conflicted. She certainly did not want to be courted by Tristan, but she did not oppose to his company. And out here, amiable friends would be few and far between.

"Why aren't you married, Isoline?" her aunt asked plainly. Isoline looked at her with her mouth slightly agape. Usually such directness would be considered rude. A topic like that was one usually beat around the bush about. Bellamira sensed Isoline's shock and continued. "At my age, one doesn't waste time stepping around topics of conversation. When one foot is in the grave, we must speak quickly before we fall in."

Isoline couldn't help but give a small sigh of relief. The rites of social niceties could be so exhausting. She was glad to have someone she could speak to with fewer constraints.

"I don't know what my father has told you—" she began, but Bellamira cut in.

"He only said that your engagement had come to a sudden sad end and you needed some time away to recover," she explained. "I thought maybe the poor chap had died or you had discovered he was a terrible rake, but you don't look like a woman who has suffered some tragedy or heartache to me."

Isoline shook her head. "No, it was nothing like that. If anything, I was the villain. Cyril loved me, and I broke his heart mercilessly."

"Why would you do that?" Bellamira asked, listening intently.

"I...I don't exactly know," she lied and hoped Bellamira didn't notice. Even though she was glad to be able to speak frankly with her aunt, she didn't think her aunt would be accepting if she admitted to ending her engagement over a dream. "I never loved him, but that was not why I ended it. I know marriage is not usually about love. But at the engagement party, I was gripped by such an abject terror, I simply couldn't go on. I felt a sudden revulsion at his touch, and I knew that if I continued with the charade, only abject misery would follow."

She looked at her aunt, expecting the woman to react harshly to such words. It made no sense for her to call off the engagement for no real reason. But she couldn't read her aunt's expression because she wasn't reacting at all. She was simply listening. She didn't even say anything during what became a very long pause in Isoline's tale. She seemed to just be waiting for Isoline to continue without prodding.

"I'm sorry," Isoline finally continued. "I must seem very ridiculous to you."

"There is nothing ridiculous about knowing your own mind, Isoline," Bellamira said. "You might not yet know why you ended things with this Cyril, and maybe you never will. But you know you couldn't marry him, and it took a lot of strength to admit that. Most girls would simply have gone on with it even when they know they shouldn't. More people should listen to that little voice of warning in the back of their mind. We'd probably all be happier for it."

Isoline nearly cried in relief. "Oh, auntie," she said. "I never thought anyone would understand me."

Bellamira stood, indicating luncheon and the conversation was at an end. "Well, I never said I understood you," she clarified. "After all, I married. I did my duty. I only never lived to regret it since..." She paused and took a pained breath. "The earl died quite soon after we married, you see."

Isoline nodded. She did not know how young Bellamira had been when her husband died, but since they did not have children, she assumed they could not have been married for long.

"He was companionate enough, but...Well, that's

enough nostalgia for today, I should think. If you don't want Tristan to call, I shall simply reply and tell him to bugger off."

"Oh, no," Isoline said. "I don't object to his company, but only as a friend. He saved my life, and he is family, of a sort. I only don't want to be expected to accept him as anything more."

"Hmm," Bellamira replied with a nod. "I see. Well, he will be here at two o'clock for tea."

"My dear cousin!" Tristan exclaimed as he crossed the room toward her. "How lovely to see you looking so...lovely!" He gripped her hands in his and kissed the back of each one excitedly.

Isoline had taken some care with her appearance. Wearing a bit of powder and lip paint and smoothing her hair. She was wearing another old-fashioned gown. Poor Jenny had been doing what she could to clean and repair Isoline's clothes, and while she had done wonders at saving many pieces, she had yet to recreate a complete outfit. Isoline feared it would only be a matter of days before she would have to ask Bellamira to provide her with a new wardrobe. While Bellamira was expected to care for her new ward, including making sure she was well-clothed, no one could have expected for her to need an entirely new retinue so soon after arriving. Even though Bellamira clearly had more money than Croesus, Isoline had no idea how miserly her aunt was, if at all. Would she balk at such an expense, or would it be nothing to her? It was a conversation Isoline preferred to put off for as long as possible.

"Tristan," Isoline said, leading him over to the same set of couches as before. When he sat, he seemed to think she would sit next to him, but she slipped her hands from his grasp and sat across from him. "I am glad to see you," she said, motioning for Talbot to serve the tea.

"And I you," he said. "I was hoping you were recovering well from your accident."

"Oh yes," Isoline said. "Quite well. My aunt is so kindly, and the staff have been quite gentle with me, making sure my every need is met."

Talbot handed a teacup and saucer with a variety of sweet and savory snacks on it to Tristan, who addressed him directly. "I am glad to hear of it, Talbot."

"Not at all, sir," Talbot said. "It is our privilege to care for the young miss."

"Do you see how they dote on me?" Isoline said as she accepted her teacup in her turn. "Talbot took such care with my books, you wouldn't know they ever spent a night in the rain."

"You enjoy reading?" Tristan asked. "Romances and poetry, no doubt," he said with a chuckle at his own joke.

"Not at all," Isoline was quick to correct him. "Oh, I enjoy the occasional romance, to be sure. But I far more enjoy the mental rigger of philosophy."

Tristan laughed again. "Aristotle? Socrates?"

"For a start," Isoline said as she sipped her tea. "But their ideas, while novel for their time, are quite rudimentary and outdated now, wouldn't you agree?"

"Oh, I don't know," Tristan replied as he fidgeted with his saucer. "It is hard to compete with the classics."

"I agree," Isoline said. "Many people don't want to argue

with convention, but I appreciate those who do, such as Adam Smith or Hildegard of Bingen. And I think Mary Wollstonecraft writes some rather shocking things, but smart truths as well. But my heart has a special place for Descartes."

"And why her?" Tristan asked as he sipped at his tea.

"You mean him?" Isoline asked helpfully.

"Oh, of course," Tristan said. "My mind was still on your affection for Mary."

Isoline nodded. "Well, Descartes wrote about dreams, something I am very interested in."

"And why is that?" he asked, though he didn't seem particularly interested as he sat back comfortably and eyed his teacup.

Isoline shrugged. "I have always had very vivid dreams. I can't help but wonder if there is any meaning to them. Descartes said, '*Et tout de même qu'un esclave qui jouissait dans le sommeil d'une liberté imaginaire, lorsqu'il commence à soupçonner que sa liberté n'est qu'un songe, craint d'être réveillé, et conspire avec ces illusions agréables pour en être plus longuement abusé, ainsi je retombe insensiblement de moi.*'"

Tristan's mouth quirked up to one side, so Isoline politely translated the quote to English.

"'I am like a prisoner who happens on enjoy an imaginary freedom in his dreams and who subsequently begins to suspect that he is asleep and, afraid of being awakened, conspires silently with his agreeable illusions,'" she said. "I think many women find a freedom in their dreams that they are unable to find in their waking hours."

"That must explain why women sleep so much," Tristan said with a laugh.

Isoline gave a polite smile but did not agree. She decided not to waste her time trying to discuss philosophy with him further. She sadly had to accept that even here in Thornrush, she would not find someone willing and able to discuss her interests.

"So where is our dear aunt?" Tristan asked as he handed his cup to Talbot.

"She should be down presently," Isoline said. "But I am glad of her delay. I wanted a chance to thank you, truly and properly, for your assistance the other night. Surely, if you had not come upon me when you did I would have died. I can never thank you enough."

"I am glad to have been of such assistance, dear cousin," he said. "But you needn't give me such credit. You may have caught a cold from being in the rain, but surely would not have died."

"No," Isoline said. "I am sure of it. In the carriage, the smoke and ash. If you hadn't..."

The parlor door opened and Bellamira entered. "Forgive the delay, nephew," Bellamira said as Tristan rose and ran over to grip her hands. "You bothered to actually send a notice of your arrival so I thought I should go to the effort of making myself presentable."

"You could wear a bag and be presentable, auntie," Tristan said as he kissed her cheek.

Bellamira moved to the couch and indicated she would like a cup of tea, which Talbot quickly brought her.

"What did I miss?" Bellamira asked.

"A rousing discussion of French philosophy," Tristan said.

"Ugh, the French," Bellamira said, shaking her head. "The less we speak of them, the better."

"I couldn't agree more," Tristan said with a laugh. "I am glad you are both here, though. I wanted to ask your permission, dear auntie, to call on Isoline more often."

"She is your cousin and you live just down the road," Bellamira said, feigning ignorance. "You can call whenever you like."

"You are too kind," he said. "But I meant in more of a... formal capacity. She has filled my mind continually since we met the other night, and I hope she may grow to fill my heart as well."

Isoline shifted uncomfortably. Even though she knew this would happen and had done her best to prepare for it, she found the right words for a response were not quick in coming.

"As I said, Tristan," she began. "I am so grateful that you happened upon me the other night. Truly, you saved my life."

"You exaggerate," he said with an exasperated sigh. "But if it will end this tedious discussion, I accept your thanks."

She nodded her appreciation. "And I am glad to have you as a neighbor and...cousin," she went on, still not comfortable equating this near stranger as family. "I am new here and there are few people in area who would make a suitable acquaintance." Even though she had come across a surprising number of people on her walk, she knew the boundaries between classes well, and she did not think her aunt would take kindly to her becoming bosom friends with the washerwomen from the creek. Finding close companions from her own social class in such a rural area would be a challenge.

"I am more than happy to fill whatever gaps there are in your life, Isoline," Tristan said as he reached across the divide and gripped her hand.

Isoline instinctively breathed in as though she had been burned and tried to pull her hand back but caught herself before delivering such an insult. "I am glad to hear of it," she said. "I so look forward to counting you among my friends."

He leaned back and released her hand, disappointment clear on his face. "Friends?" he asked.

Isoline nodded. "A dear friend," she restated.

"Ah, I see," he said as he stood.

"I do hope I have not offended you," Isoline said quickly as she stood as well.

"No, no, of course not," he said as he tried to mask his discomfort. "After all, what are family members but very good friends? I think I shall take my leave." He moved toward the door, but then stopped and looked back at her.

"I hope you do not think me too forward, cousin," he said. "But I feel that in the new spirit of friendship I should say something. I heard that you came across that indolent tenant, Auberon Drochia."

At just the mention of his name, Isoline felt a rush of heat in her chest. She only prayed it did not reach her face.

"I...happened upon many of the tenants of the estate yesterday," she quickly said. "But I believe he was one them."

"Our aunt, because of her kind heart and out of respect for his family, allows him to remain on the property," he said.

"How dare you say such a thing about my heart!" Bellamira snapped.

"Be that as it may," Tristan continued, "I feel it is my duty to warn you that the man is a rake and of no quality. It would be best to steer well clear of him."

Isoline pressed her lips and nodded. Of course she had been foolish to think that she would have any freedom from having a controlling man in her life by being hundreds of miles from her father.

"You are...so kind," Isoline finally managed through a tight smile. "I will give your words the full weight of measure they deserve."

"That is all I ask," he said as he gave a quick short bow and then left the parlor.

Isoline squeezed her hands together tightly and waited for her anger to cool before returning to her seat across from her aunt.

"I suppose the full weight of that measure is none at all?" her aunt inquired with a raised brow as she sipped her tea.

Isoline smiled in relief. "I meant what I said about not wanting to find a suitor," she said. "Please don't think I did anything to jeopardize my reputation with Mr. Drochia. It was truly an accident that we met yesterday and we barely exchanged a few words before I quickly excused myself."

Bellamira shook her head. "I know Auberon quite well," she said. "He is a perfect gentleman. I have no concerns about that."

"Thank you for understanding," Isoline said.

"I may be old, and I may have been a widow for many years, but men never change," Bellamira said. "If anything, the man to worry about will be Tristan. If he has his eye on you, I doubt he will give up that easily."

Isoline wrung her hands again. She had a feeling her aunt was right.

CHAPTER SIX

*I*soline was relieved that Tristan did not call on her again over the next several days. He did send her a book of French poetry, which she accepted gladly. He might not have been interested in or understood what she had told him the other day, but at least he had listened... somewhat. She sent him a note thanking him for the thoughtful gift and reiterated her appreciation for their friendship.

She was settling comfortably into her new life. Every day, after Bess helped her wash and dress, she would eat breakfast and then head out for a walk. She knew better than to walk quite so far as the first time and rarely left the confines of the estate proper. She was disappointed that she did not come across Auberon again, but knew it was probably for the best if she wished to keep to her resolve to allow no man to court her.

She would then spend the rest of the morning reading while she waited for her aunt to join her for luncheon. The two would embroider together, read, chat, and play cards until dinner. After which the two would usually enjoy a small glass of port before retiring to their own quarters for the evening to do what they willed.

It was a gentle, easy life, and Isoline was happy to be living it for the time being. She knew that eventually she would get terribly bored and need to find something more taxing to keep her from climbing the walls, but she had only been at Thornrush for less than two weeks and imagined she was on a sort of restful holiday.

But her holiday ended when she received a letter from Royston.

My dearest sister,

I do hope you are enjoying your new placement at Thornrush Manor. Please do give Grand-Aunt Bellamira the kindest regards from her nephews and nieces-in-law. Geraldine and Eunice miss you terribly and wax endlessly on the silence through the house caused by your absence. Though I believe that silence will soon be shattered by the cries of a new baby in the house. Eunice announced at dinner last night that she and our brother Lawrence are finally expecting their first child. I had hoped to be the one to inform you of the happy news, but Eunice told me you had already discovered the situation of your own accord before you left. You always were a clever one.

Speaking of children, Henry Marsdale, the highly acclaimed tutor, has agreed to take my eldest son, Oliver, as a student. As you can imagine, this is quite an honor, and could do so much for his future. However, all our dreams were nearly shattered when he made his salary requirements clear. My darling, I should have become a teacher! I dare say my own professors at university did not earn such a pay in their life, much less a year. Well, we do not have to give him an answer immediately, but he will require one before the fall. I hope we will be able to give him the response we all desire.

I do hope you and Aunt Bellamira are getting along well,
and I hope to hear back from you soon.
Sincerely,
Your devoted brother,
Royston.

Isoline nearly rent the letter in two in frustration. Always were the clever one, indeed! If she had an ounce of sense she could see through her brother's pleasant correspondence for what it truly was—a reminder that her true purpose at Thornrush Manor was to fleece an inheritance out of her elderly aunt.

Of course, if Bellamira did leave her an inheritance, she would be happy to accept it, but she didn't want to...*seduce* it out of her, for lack of a better phrase. She was grateful that her grand-aunt had taken her in, and was truly enjoying her life here. She did not want to taint that by acting like some sort of treasure hunter.

At the same time, she knew that her family expected it of her. They wanted her to do her utmost to become Bellamira's heir not to help herself, but the whole family. The same as her marriage to Cyril was not for her own benefit, but to the benefit of the family. She was not a sole human tossed about on an empty sea. She was a daughter, a sister, an aunt. She was a member of a family, and she needed to play her proper role.

And it certainly was an honor that Mr. Marsdale had agreed to tutor Oliver. Mr. Marsdale had been a tutor to the princes when they were young, but instead of tutoring the next generation of royals, he had become an itinerant tutor due to his belief that all young men, not just the nobility, deserved a quality education. As far as she knew, Mr. Marsdale did not extend such beliefs to educating girls, but for a boy like Oliver, such a tutor could indeed change his life. If she could help finance his education, she would. She took a deep breath and steeled herself for spending the afternoon ingratiating herself to her grand-aunt.

"*I* won again," Bellamira declared as she placed the winning card on the table.

Isoline sighed in frustration. "This is becoming quite tedious." She had just lost three games in a row to Bellamira, only the first one intentionally.

"Oh, this whole day is becoming rather tedious, don't you think?" Bellamira asked as she collected the cards and straightened them to replace them in their card sleeve.

"I have been enjoying my time here, auntie," Isoline said. "But I have been wondering if I should find something more productive to do with my time."

"Such as?" Bellamira asked.

"I have no idea," Isoline said. "Most of my education centered around keeping house, of course. Sewing, a bit of cooking. Just enough reading to make conversation but not so much to appear dull. But all of that was to prepare for marriage and a family. Now that neither is on the table, I'm not quite sure how to occupy my time."

"Yes," Bellamira said. "I can see how life in the country could be quite boring for a young woman."

"How have you kept your mind sharp all these years you have lived alone?" Isoline asked.

"Oh, well I have never lived truly alone," Bellamira said.

"I have more staff than I can count, not to mention the other matters of the estate."

"I would love to learn more about that," Isoline said. "It must be so complicated to run a house like this. Almost like a large business."

"Not only like one, but actually one," Bellamira said as she stood and walked to a large window that looked out over the rolling hills of the land around the estate. "I employ more people than most private companies in London. As do most of the upper nobility. Combined, the aristocracy employs a third of the British workforce."

Isoline felt her jaw drop. "I had no idea."

"Most people don't," Bellamira said. "All this talk in the papers about abolishing the monarchy and turning out the private houses. Foolishness. Thousands of good British folk would find themselves out of work, out of home, out of food, the whole country would be out of order, much like the French were half a century ago. Many of us can still remember those days."

Isoline realized that her grand-auntie indeed was as old as she claimed if she could still remember the French Revolution.

"Even though it was happening across the channel, it must have been so frightening to hear of what was happening," Isoline said.

"Indeed, it was," Bellamira said with a nod. "But thankfully such radical ideals never took root here. I know some people still wax poetic about such a utopia without landowners and peasants, but there is a natural order to everything in the world. God made it so. High and low, rich and poor. We all have a place and a part to play."

Isoline wasn't quite sure about all that. She thought about her own lack of education simply because she was a girl and how much she resented it. She imagined the poor must also feel slighted for being born into a life they had no control over and then seemingly punished for it for the whole of their existence. But Isoline kept her opinions to herself since she didn't want to argue with her aunt and risk upsetting her.

"Still, you must have had some hobby or passion to keep you occupied?" she tried. "Surely managing the estate doesn't take up all of your time."

"Well, I do have a soft spot for art," Bellamira said.

"I've noticed," Isoline said. "Just walking the halls here is like being in an art museum. You have so many exquisite pieces."

"You should see the bedrooms," Bellamira said with a chuckle. "Some rooms don't have any furniture in them, just four walls of paintings and then stacks of them on the floors."

"I'd love to, but I'm afraid I can't," Isoline explained. "I tried a few of the other doors on my floor, but they are all locked."

"Oh!" Bellamira exclaimed. "That's right! I forget because if I need something I just send for Talbot. But we do keep the unused rooms locked, isn't that right, Talbot?"

"That's right, your ladyship," Talbot said, and Isoline nearly started. She was getting so used to having him stand quietly in the background whenever Bellamira was around she nearly forgot he was there.

"Can you bring an extra key for Isoline?" Bellamira asked.

"Of course, your ladyship," he said and silently slipped out of the room.

"I actually have a new painting arriving soon," Bellamira said. "I have a buyer, over on the continent. She goes to auctions and estate sales for me and visits with new up and coming artists. When she sees a piece she thinks I will like, she buys it for me and ships it over."

"You employ a woman to buy art for you?" Isoline asked, surprised and confused. She had never heard of such a job.

"Oh yes," Bellamira said. "I'm very lucky to have her since I...well, I could never get over there on my own."

"Have you not traveled, auntie?" Isoline asked. "No family to tie you down here and surely plenty of money. You must have traveled extensively."

Bellamira frowned and looked back out the window as she fiddled with her collar. "Yes, I suppose I should have," she said sadly.

Isoline realized that Bellamira had not once left the house since she had arrived, not even opened a window. She wondered if Bellamira was a recluse. It was possible. She had everything she needed delivered or taken care of by her staff. Isoline realized she had made a terrible blunder, but she wasn't sure how to recover. Thankfully, Talbot returned at that moment.

"I have found a key, your ladyship," he announced.

Bellamira's face brightened as she walked to him and took the key. "Thank you so much, Talbot." He gave a small bow and backed away. Bellamira then motioned for Isoline to follow her.

"I'll show you the first room, then you can explore on your own," Bellamira explained as she ascended the stairs. "Feel free to take note of three or four paintings you like and we can have them placed in your room."

"That would be wonderful," Isoline said. "It would make my room more my own."

"Exactly," Bellamira said. They turned down the hallway

toward Isoline's room but stopped at the first door. Bellamira slipped the key into the lock and opened the door with ease. Isoline had no idea how often the doors were used, but she was surprised when the hinges didn't so much as squeak.

The room was quite dark, so Isoline walked over and pulled open the curtains, sending a swirl of dust motes into the air, which she swished away from her face. When she turned around, she was indeed shocked at the number of paintings that greeted her. There must have been dozens in this room alone! Every space on the wall held a painting, and indeed there were several on the floor leaning against the wall and furniture as though waiting for an available space to open up.

Like the ones she had seen in the hallway, the pieces here were an eclectic mix. British, French, Greek, and oriental designs all stood side by side as though attending the most fascinating garden party.

"I know," Bellamira said. "You must think I have a terrible addiction."

"Oh no," Isoline said as she surveyed several paintings while not moving from one spot. "It is a marvelous collection! I don't think I will be able to choose only three or four for my rooms."

"Well choose a dozen," Bellamira said. "We can rotate them out every season."

"Is every room in house like this?" Isoline asked.

"Well, not every room," Bellamira said. "We have some guestrooms that are only home to a few artfully placed pieces and a few other rooms for other functions. But, yes, most of the rooms in the house are probably as cluttered with art as this one."

"It will take me forever just to look at each one," Isoline

said. "I am certain this will keep my mind busy for the fore-seeable future."

"I am glad to hear it," Bellamira said. "We can talk about your favorite pieces at dinner. Speaking of which, I need to speak with the cook. I'll leave you to your exploring, dear."

Isoline happily spent the next hour looking at every piece in the room, and when she was done, she was excited to move on to the next one. She wondered if there was any sort of cataloging system. She would never remember which ones were her favorites or where to find them without some sort of notation. She went to her room and grabbed a notebook and pencil before moving on to the next room.

She decided to be as orderly as possible about it and went all the way to the end of the hallway. The sun was setting and the servants didn't bother to light the lamps down the unused hall, so it was a bit dark, but she went to the very last door and used her key to open it.

As expected, the room was dark. She crossed to the window and threw open the blinds. When she turned around, she nearly screamed and dropped her notebook.

She was looking at herself.

Her heart beat furiously in her chest, and it was only after she willed herself to breathe did she realize she was looking at the portrait her mother must have sent to Bellamira many years before.

She was not sure why the painting unnerved her, but she thought it must have simply been the surprise of seeing her own face where she did not expect it. But there was also something slightly...off about the painting, but she wasn't sure what. She took a step closer to it to get a better look.

The girl in the painting had the same nose, the same cheekbones, the same chin that she remembered. She had the same full dark hair that was pulled back into tight curls. But there was something different about the eyes. The eyes looking back at her were not her own. At that, she realized the color was wrong. While her eyes were a deep doe brown, the eyes of the girl in the painting were bright blue.

They were the eyes of her aunt.

Isoline had noticed a familiarity in Bellamira's face when they first met, but she hadn't realized just how similar they looked. Of course, Bellamira was nearly seventy years older than Isoline, but still, the similarities were striking and she was surprised she had never noticed it before.

She shook her head and turned away, the painting of a young woman who looked so much like herself and yet was not her too jarring to continue starring at. Yet when she turned, she was met with yet *another* rendition of herself. This one, though, she recognized. This one *was* her. It had to have been the painting her mother sent to Bellamira on her behalf.

She took the painting of herself and set it next to the painting of Bellamira. She certainly wasn't imagining it. As she looked at the painting of herself from merely six years ago alongside the painting of a young Bellamira, the likenesses could not be ignored. Other than the color of the eyes and the style of clothes, the girls in the paintings could have been sisters.

More than that, they could have been twins.

PART II

Deep into that darkness peering, long I stood
there, wondering, fearing,
Doubting, dreaming dreams no mortal ever
dared to dream before.

~ Edgar Allan Poe

CHAPTER SEVEN

A loud knock reverberated through the walls of Thornrush Manor. Isoline, who had been lounging with a book in the parlor, raised her head curiously. She had been at Thornrush for many weeks, but there had not been a single visitor aside from Tristan, at least not one who used the front door. The postman, the delivery boys, the staff who did not live in the main house, they all used the servants' entrance with a little bell. A knock at the front door was an event, indeed.

Isoline moved to a room at the front of the house and looked out a window at the black carriage parked in front. The sight of the carriage sent her heart to fluttering as she recalled her accident. She had not even seen a carriage since her arrival—she had not gone anywhere that required one—so she was surprised the sight of one gave her such a flash of anxiety.

The two large, black horses pulling the carriage stomped their feet and made excited noises as one of the grooms treated them to apples. These horses were happy, yet the panicked whinnies of the horses who had pulled her carriage assaulted her ears.

Her breathing became short and quick. She wanted to get away, yet she could not move. She knew she was near to fainting, yet she could not look away...

"Isoline!" Bellamira called, breaking into Isoline's thoughts.

Her aunt's voice pulled Isoline from the brink of terror and back to the safety of the parlor.

"Y-yes, auntie?" Isoline asked as she slipped away from the window and toward the door.

Bellamira waved for her to follow her. "Come, come! It has arrived!"

A middle-aged man in a dark suit was handing a long package to Talbot.

"It wasn't easy getting this out," the man said. "The whole area is tense, dangerous right now. War is coming, Talbot, I can tell you that."

"Indeed, sir," Talbot said, holding the package gingerly.

"War?" Isoline asked. "There is a war coming?"

"Oh, nothing for you to worry about, love," the man said as he removed his hat and slicked his hair back. "Damn Russians and Turks, they'll get what's coming to them in the end, you'll see."

Isoline then realized he was referencing the rising tension in eastern Europe. She had not been following the problem in the newspapers too closely. Russia and the Ottoman Empire were far away and the two countries had been fighting over religious matters, something Isoline didn't bother herself with overmuch. But what did that have to do with the mysterious delivery?

"Matteo," Bellamira said with a smile as she approached the man with her hand extended.

"Duchess!" the man exclaimed as he eagerly accepted her hand and kissed the back of it. "You look younger every time I see you."

Bellamira giggled like a school girl at Matteo's flattery. "Matteo, may I introduce my niece, Isoline," she said as she motioned Isoline forward.

"Yes, you certainly may," he said lasciviously as he took Isoline's hand and kissed the back of it as well.

She smiled politely but pulled her hand back as soon as he loosened his grip enough for her to do so.

"I hope you didn't have much trouble bringing me the painting," Bellamira said to Matteo.

"Well, I like to gripe, but it wasn't too bad. This time anyway. You should tell Miss Ezerbet to get out of there, though. Why can't she find pieces somewhere safer, or warmer, to hunt for your art, like Florence."

Bellamira waved him off. "That's exactly why she is there. She must liberate as much as she can in case the area ends up cordoned off if war breaks out."

Isoline's eyes wandered to the doors on the second-floor gallery and she thought about all those beautiful paintings locked away in dark rooms for decades, seen and appreciated by no one. Not her idea of liberty, but she held her tongue.

"True enough, I suppose," Matteo said. "Well, I better be off. I promised the missus a trip to Bath while we're in country." He replaced his hat and turned toward the door.

"Oh, but don't you want to see what you went to such lengths to procure for me?" Bellamira asked.

"Oh, I saw it," he said. "Ezerbet showed me when I picked it up and we repackaged it for travel. Not my thing. Damn creepy, really. But whatever makes you happy, duchess."

"Oh, it does," Bellamira purred like a cat with a bowl of cream. "Thank you so much for your assistance."

"Anytime, duchess," he said as he doffed his hat and breezed back out the door.

"He was an...interesting character, auntie," Isoline said.

"Well, he's Italian, what can you say?" Bellamira asked as she turned to Talbot and her treasure. Having not known many Italians—or any—Isoline couldn't reply. "Let's have a look," Bellamira said to Talbot.

"Yes, your ladyship," he said as he and James worked together to open the package.

"You are in for quite a treat, my darling," Bellamira told Isoline as she rubbed her hands together. "All the way from Romania! That's about a far east as you can go before you fall into the Orient."

Isoline sighed and thought about what an exciting life Miss Ezerbet must lead, chasing down art all over the world.

Talbot finally held the canvas up and unfurled the painting for all to see.

Isoline gasped and held her hand to her mouth.

It was horrifying.

"Exquisite! Exquisite!" Bellamira exclaimed, clapping her hands and laughing like a school girl.

A woman in a white gown with long blonde hair laid prostrate on her bed on a coverlet of scarlet, her head and curls dangling dangerously over the edge. Her arms stretched out above her. She would have fallen off if not for the horrifying beast that sat on her stomach, leering at her with buggy eyes and bulbous nose. Blood red drapes hung behind her, and peeking out from them was a black horse with white eyes.

"A-a-auntie..." was the only sound Isoline could utter.

Her throat was closed with shock. She couldn't imagine anyone painting such a horrid image, much less paying the enormous sum her aunt must have spent not only on the painting, but on Ezerbet's services and Matteo's delivery fee.

"I know," Bellamira said, shaking her head reverently. "Most incredible. Have you ever seen the like of it?"

"I...most certainly have not," Isoline said truthfully. She shuddered and started to turn away, glad the bestial painting would soon be locked away, never to see the light of day again.

"After I have it framed," Bellamira mused, "I think I will place it right here in the foyer." She walked over to one of the walls opposite the front door and indicated a space where a traditional portrait of a man now hung.

Isoline walked over and looked at the portrait. "Now, auntie," she said. "I am not sure..." She squinted to read the name. "Henry, the Second Earl of Payne, would appreciate his place being usurped."

"Oh, he was a dreadful old sot," Bellamira said. "He never liked me. He's lucky to be here in the house at all."

"Still," Isoline said, trying again. "When people come to a grand old estate like this one, they will expect to see portraits of former residents. It's tradition. I'm sure we can find another place for the new one."

"Hmm," Bellamira said, squeezing her chin as she thought. "Perhaps you are right. Perhaps the parlor."

Isoline's heart dropped and she did her best to suppress a disappointed sigh. She was not sure which was worse— seeing the monstrosity whenever she walked in the door or having it hang over her while she tried to carry on conversations. She decided to drop the subject. She was obviously not going to be able to dissuade her aunt from displaying it somewhere in the house.

"Whatever makes you happy, auntie," Isoline said with a smile and turned away to resume her book in the sitting room.

"Well, I'll have time to consider it," Bellamira said. "First, it will need to be framed. Isoline, dear, could you take the painting to Auberon for me."

Isoline started, not sure which part of the sentence shocked her more. "Auberon?" she asked about first. "What does he have to do with anything?"

"He's an artist," Bellamira explained. "And he does the framework for his own pieces and any I procure.

"He's an artist?" Isoline asked, dumbfounded.

"Of course," Bellamira said. "What did you think he did on the estate?"

"I've barely spoken to him," Isoline said. "I thought he was just another tenant farmer."

Bellamira let out a bark of a laugh. "Farmer? Auberon? Never! He hasn't the stomach for such physical labor. He's a dreamer. A poet, but with a brush."

Isoline shrugged. "We only spoke for a moment. I really had no idea."

"Well, we shall put that to rights," Bellamira said as she walked over to Talbot and asked him to roll up the painting. "You can take the painting to him after luncheon. He will know what to do with it. His cottage is not far from here and I'm sure you will enjoy the walk." She then walked over and offered the rolled-up canvas to Isoline.

Isoline did her best to still her quaking fingers as she held her hands out to accept the painting. She didn't even want to be in the same room with it, much less touch the thing. The only comfort she took was in the fact that it would soon be out of the house, if only for a little while.

*A*s Isoline followed her aunt's directions to reach Auberon's cottage, she felt butterflies in her stomach. She was excited to see him again and glad she would be able to talk to him and not worry about having to excuse herself hastily, but she knew the man was a danger to her resolve to remain unattached. Not that her father would ever approve such a match. From what Bellamira told her, Auberon had little money and no title or property. He was a good artist, but not a rich or famous one. And he had no driving ambition to be much more than he was. He was happy to create his art and live simply. And while Isoline could find no fault with the desire to live a simple life, she knew her father would.

She shook her head at thinking such foolish thoughts. Who was even thinking of marriage! She had barely said two words to the man weeks ago. She was being ridiculous.

As she crested a hill along the well-worn path, she was able to look down on Auberon's cottage and the scene it overlooked.

It was breathtaking.

The thatched-roof cottage sat on the hillside overlooking the sea. The waves crashed upon the shore and the emerald grass glistened in the sun. A small rock wall wended its way along the property and a few large oak trees stood here and there. It was a perfect blend of peace, serenity, and majesty. She suddenly understood why Auberon would be perfectly content in this spot.

As she stood, reveling in the view, the door to the

cottage opened and Auberon stepped out. He took a few steps forward and placed his hands on his hips as he surveyed the scene before him. He held his head up and took in a deep breath of the salty sea air and his long dark hair fluttered in the breeze. Isoline watched him in surprise. He must see this view every day of his life, yet he still appreciated it. She shifted and accidentally knocked a small stone loose, which audibly rolled down the hillside. Auberon looked her way and gave her a large smile. She smiled in return as warmth replaced the butterflies in her stomach. He raised a hand in greeting as he walked up the path toward her.

"Miss Beresford," he said. "So lovely to see you again."

She gave him a small nod of her head. "Please, we are neighbors. You must call me Isoline."

She did not think it was possible, but his smile grew even bigger at her world.

"I will do that, Isoline," he said, and her chest swelled.

She cleared her throat and looked out over the view. "It is stunning," she said. "I had no idea the estate housed such sights."

"It never grows old," he said as he turned around and looked back at the sea. "I could live a thousand years and still lose my breath when I opened that door."

"Have you tried to paint it?" Isoline asked. "My aunt says you are an artist. You must find the view to be quite inspiring."

He turned back to her. "I could never do it justice. Your aunt must speak far too kindly of me."

Isoline held out the box with the dreaded painting. "She rarely speaks kindly of anyone, but you are one of the lucky few."

He laughed as he took the offered package. "Ah, she mentioned she had a new piece coming. Have you seen it?"

Isoline tried to hide a grimace but knew she had failed when Auberon laughed again.

"That bad?" he asked.

"Art is...subjective," she said. "Isn't that what they say? Who am I to judge?"

"Still, I'll have to make sure my frame outshines the painting," he said. "Would that suit you?"

She sighed in appreciation. "That would be wonderful. Anything to draw the eye away from the horrid beast that dominates the image now."

"Have no fear, dear Isoline," he said gallantly. "I will do my best to please you."

"You are too kind," she said. "Do you know when it will be ready?"

"A couple of months, I should think," he said. "I make the frames from scratch, starting with timber from trees right here on the estate. I'll have to look at the painting and see what sort of wood I should start with, how big a piece I will need...I'm sorry. I'm probably boring you."

"Not at all," she said. "I enjoy hearing people speak on the things they are passionate about. It is amazing how even a piece of wood can bring such a light to your eyes."

"And what of you, dear Isoline?" he asked. "What brings a spark to your eyes?"

Dreams, she wanted to say, but held back. Every conversation she had ever had with a man regarding the nature of dreams only lead to disappointment. She didn't want to be disappointed by Auberon. Not yet. She wanted to enjoy the fantasy of him for a little while longer.

"I...suppose I am still trying to discover that for myself," she finally said.

"There is a...true loveliness about you when you are deep in thought," he said, and she blushed. "I first noticed it when I found you sitting under the tree all those weeks ago. Your face was so...serene. Pensive."

"How long were you watching me?" she asked.

"Not nearly long enough," he said. He took a step closer and looked down at her, deep into her eyes. She should have stepped back, but she did not. She felt as though she could get lost in such eyes, as deep and dark as her own.

"Isoline?" he asked in a husky whisper.

"Yes?" she softly replied.

"Would you let me paint you?" he asked.

"Oh," was all she managed at first. She tore her eyes away and stepped back. The memory of seeing the painting of her aunt so like herself still unnerved her. She had not been back to the room since and was not sure she would return. She hadn't even been exploring the other rooms as much as she had originally planned because she was worried about what else she might find. While she realized she should be flattered that Auberon wanted to paint a portrait of her, the very idea made her too uncomfortable to acquiesce.

"No," she finally said. "I...I don't think so. I'm sure there are many things more beautiful or interesting than me you could recreate with your brush. Like...that squirrel over there." She pointed to a scurrying critter on the ground by one of the trees.

He looked over at the squirrel and chuckled. "I doubt that squirrel has eyes nearly as expressive as yours."

"Still," she said, a bit embarrassed. "I am afraid I must decline."

"Of course," he said. "Forgive me for asking."

"Already done," she said. "But perhaps one day you could show me some of your work?"

"I would be more than delighted," he said. "If you ever want to know more about art or if you would like a painting lesson, let me know."

"Actually," Isoline said. "My aunt, she has...hundreds, possibly thousands of paintings throughout the house."

He nodded. "I am aware. She is quite the avid collector."

"Yes," Isoline said. "She has given me permission to examine her collection and choose a few for myself. But it has been quite overwhelming. Do you think you could tell me more about some of the pieces and help me choose the best ones?"

"As you said, art is subjective," he said. "You might personally enjoy a painting by an unknown hermit living on the sea more than one by William Blake."

She grimaced and did not try to hide it. "I dare say I would dread having a Blake in my quarters."

He laughed. "Exactly. But I know what you mean. I can certainly use my artist's eye to help you choose a few paintings for your rooms."

"What would be wonderful," she said, nearly hopping in excitement.

"Is there a particular time you would prefer me to call?" he asked.

"My schedule is rather open," Isoline said. "Other than you and my cousin Tristan, I've barely met a soul."

"I hope to see you again soon then, dear Isoline," he said with a bow.

Isoline turned back up the path with a spring in her step and thoughts of Auberon in her heart.

CHAPTER EIGHT

I soline...

He had been coming to her almost every night for weeks. But for the first time, she was feeling apprehensive about it.

She knew it was because of Auberon.

She grabbed her robe as she stood and waited for him to come to her. Together, they walked in silence through the glen in the cool blue night.

She felt content and safe in his company, and something more. She truly believed that she would never need a living man in her life as long as she had the man in her dreams.

So why couldn't she stop thinking about Auberon?

She knew it was because settling for a figment of her imagination was foolish. Auberon was a real, flesh-and-blood man. A handsome man. A thoughtful man. A man who said more to her than just her name but carried a conversation.

She already felt a stronger, deeper connection to Auberon than she had ever felt for Cyril. She had agreed to marry Cyril because it was the right thing to do. But

Auberon ignited in her something she never thought she would have if she married a man out of duty.

Passion.

She knew that even thinking about such a thing was dangerous. As she had already told herself a hundred times, she would never be allowed to marry Auberon. So entertaining any thoughts of getting closer to him, getting to know him, allowing him close to her...It could only lead to disaster.

She did not know what the future held. Her aunt could die at any moment and leave her with nothing. Her father might arrange a marriage without her consent. She might need to enter a convent to keep from becoming a woman of the street. Her virtue, her honor, her dignity needed to remain above reproach. She could need it later.

She felt guilty about all these thoughts running through her head as she walked alone at night with the man in her dreams. Did he have any idea what she was thinking? What she was going through? She rather thought not. He had been angry and left her when she told him about Cyril. If he knew about her budding feelings for Auberon, how could he be anything but upset. Especially after he helped calm her when she thought she was out of options. He might have even had a hand in arranging her situation here with her aunt.

She sighed and shook her head. She felt something brush against the back of her right hand as it dangled at her side. She didn't look, but turned the tips of her fingers out and entangled them in his. He was there. He was real. She didn't know how it was possible, but the man in her dreams was every bit as real as Auberon. And just like with Cyril, she would eventually have to make a choice.

But not tonight.

*T*here was a knock at the door. Isoline's heart leaped into her throat, but she did not rise from her chair. She did not want Auberon to think she was too eager to see him, even though she had been sure to wear her nicest outfit and fix her hair just right and wear just a bit of makeup in case he should stop by.

The door to the sitting room opened and Talbot announced the visitor. "The Vicar Edwards."

Isoline nearly dropped her book as she stood, she was so surprised. In breezed a man who appeared to be in his late thirties with rosy cheeks and a smile on his face. He removed his hat and walked over to Isoline with his hand extended.

"My dear Miss Beresford," he said as he gave her hand a congenial shake. "Please do forgive me for taking so long to call. It is a pleasure to finally meet you."

It took a moment for Isoline to find the words to respond. "Think nothing of it," she said. "I had no idea I should have expected you. Talbot, tea please."

"Of course, miss," he said as he left the room momentarily to prepare the tray.

Isoline did not bother to mention her aunt. She was sure the staff had already alerted her to their guest. She motioned to the couches and they sat across from each other.

"To what do I owe such an esteemed visit?" Isoline asked.

"I truly must apologize," the vicar said. "I have known

about your arrival for weeks, but it is rather a long way out and I simply couldn't carve out the time to visit until today."

"There is nothing to apologize for, truly," Isoline said. "As you say, we are rather isolated. I am glad to have a visit even if it is only in a blue moon."

"Yes," he said. "My wife also wanted to come, but trying to find time for *both* of us was proving rather impossible. She couldn't come today because she didn't think the children could behave for a carriage ride here and back again and be quiet long enough for a decent chat." He let out a chuckle.

Isoline was glad to hear of him speak about his family. Even though he was complaining, she could tell it was good-natured and that he adored his wife and children. She was relieved to have one man she could speak with without being concerned that he would suddenly try to be more than friends. Though she would have been glad to have another woman around to speak with. While she enjoyed the peace and quiet of the house initially, she was starting to miss the sisterly friendship of Geraldine and Eunice.

"I will have to make it a point to visit your home soon, then," Isoline said as Talbot returned with the tea tray. "I am sure your wife would appreciate the company."

"Indeed!" he said, brightening even more, if it were possible. "She rarely gets out, between taking care of the girls and managing the home and helping me with sermons. The poor woman is run ragged, but I could not have asked for a better helpmate."

"You are truly blessed," Isoline said.

Talbot handed them both cups of tea and they sipped at them before continuing.

"So, how are you adjusting to life in the country?" the vicar asked. "Must be terribly quiet to you."

Isoline nodded. "I quite welcomed it at first. My two elder brothers and their wives and their children all lived with my father and myself, so we had a rather lively home. The peace and quiet of Thornrush was a welcome respite. And I do so enjoy the company of my aunt. But, yes, I have been looking for something more to occupy my time lately."

"You should come to church this Sunday," he said, leaping right into a conversation Isoline thought they would dance around for much longer. She nearly spilled her tea in surprise.

"Oh! Well...you see, of course..." she stammered, but thankfully she was interrupted by the arrival of her aunt.

"Vicar Edwards," Bellamira said as she walked over and held out her hand. The vicar warmly squeezed both of his hands around hers and gave her a small bow in greeting. "Forgive me for making you wait," she said as they all got comfortable again. "I trust my niece was taking good care of you."

"Of course!" he exclaimed. "She was just telling me how peaceful Thornrush Manor is."

Bellamira chuckled. "I am sure she is just being polite. For an old woman like me, it is perfect. But for a young woman...Well, let's just say I can see her mind beginning to atrophy."

The three of them laughed together.

"Now, auntie," Isoline said. "That's not exactly true. Have you seen my aunt's art collection, vicar? It is brilliant! They have given me much to think about."

"I have seen some of them," he said with a nod. "In fact, some of the pieces we have at the church and in the vicarage were donated by Lady Granville. Back when my father was the vicar here."

"Oh yes," Bellamira said with a nod. "Your father was a

frequent visitor here for many years. His passing was a great loss to the community."

"I feel I will never fill his shoes," the vicar said solemnly.

"When he spoke," Bellamira said, "the whole building would shake! You could feel his words reverberate into the depths of your soul. Well, I can honestly say that I would not be the God-fearing woman I am today if not for him."

"I am glad to hear that," the vicar said. "He wanted nothing more than to save the souls of those who would otherwise be damned."

Isoline nearly choked on her tea. "Vicar!" she said. "Surely my aunt didn't have a...a damned soul."

"Oh!" he said, placing his hand to his heart. "My apologies, my dear! I didn't mean to imply any such thing. Do forgive me. But anyone who knew my father, your aunt included, would understand my meaning. It was simply his style. Anyone who didn't live up to his exacting standards."

"The *Lord's* standards," Bellamira added in.

"Of course," he said with a small nod, but Isoline thought he didn't quite agree.

"That must have been a difficult way to grow up," Isoline said. "I can relate, on a certain level."

"I'm sure you can," the vicar said. "There is a lot of pressure on young ladies to act a certain way and dress a certain way. So many rules, most of which are unspoken. Even my poor wife has to deal with such excruciating details. All the time she has to spend on clothes, and flowers, and notes, and the like. And she already has a husband! I dread the world my daughters will be growing up in, always scared to make the slightest mistake or risk not being able to marry just the right man at just the right time and have just the right wedding." He shuddered as he shook his head.

"Quite," Isoline said, surprised to find such a sympathetic soul in a man.

"I can agree that some of these new 'social niceties' that seem to have developed over the last couple of decades are extreme," Bellamira said. "But when it comes to the rules He has laid down, they are a protection. They are the only way to guide the soul to Heaven."

"Of course," the vicar said. "His Word is the only book of manners we truly need." He and Isoline laughed, both wanting to lighten the conversation, but Bellamira seemed to not be finished quite yet.

"Hell and damnation," she said. "That is the only path for those who do not follow His laws."

"Now, Lady Granville," the vicar said gently. "He is also a God of great forgiveness and compassion. We all make mistakes. I would rather welcome any into the flock with an open and contrite heart than drive out those who fall short."

"Your father would disagree," Bellamira snapped. "Are you rejecting his legacy?"

"I am grateful for all my father taught me," he said with a surprising gentleness Isoline did not think she would have in his situation. "But he and I did not always see eye to eye on every interpretation. His was a God of vengeance; mine is a God of love."

Isoline had never been much of a religious person. She had gone to church every Sunday as she should when she was growing up and believed in God, but she was not obsessed with the Bible and religion overmuch. Instead of going home to read her Bible, she would leave it on the table untouched until the next Sunday, opting instead to read something rather unsuitable for a woman she had pinched from her brothers' school satchel.

But the way Vicar Edwards spoke of God in such a gentle and loving manner did appeal to her, and she was quite surprised by how irritating Bellamira seemed to find it. While she originally wanted to make an excuse about why she couldn't visit the church, she now thought maybe she would enjoy it. Not so much for any religious discussion, but to make friends and have a mentally challenging discussion. If Vicar Edwards was this sympathetic and open-minded, his wife could be just the sort of companion she was looking for.

"There is only one God," Bellamira said firmly, her thin hands nearly shaking in anger. The vicar was no longer smiling and seemed to fidget in his seat.

"Vicar Edwards," Isoline broke in. "Earlier you invited me to church this Sunday. I think I should take you up on the offer."

He smiled and sighed in relief at Isoline's words, and Isoline thought he was silently thanking her with his eyes.

"I look forward to it, Miss Beresford," he said as he stood. "I am afraid I have stayed much longer than I should. My wife will be anxious for my return to help take the children for an outing. Like little puppies, the lot of them. If they do not have their daily exercise, we all pay the price."

Isoline laughed at the vicar's words and stood to escort him to the front door, squeezing his hand in friendship as he left.

When she returned to the sitting room, Bellamira was standing at the mantel, looking into the fireplace as though lost in deep thought.

"Auntie?" Isoline asked. "Would you care to accompany me to church on Sunday? I think the fresh air may be good for you."

Bellamira looked up at Isoline, and Isoline nearly

gasped. Her aunt's eyes looked dull and watery, as though she had aged many years in only the few moments she had been gone.

"It is too late for me...for us..." Bellamira said as she left the room, walking slowly and carefully.

Like an old woman.

*I*soline did not see her aunt for the rest of the day or the next morning before she left for church. She had to leave quite early since it took her about an hour to arrive, but the grooms who prepared the carriage and the coachman who agreed to accompany her did not grumble in the slightest and seemed almost pleased for an excuse to go to town. Even Bess donned her best outfit and eagerly agreed to accompany Isoline. They decided they would make a day of it, having luncheon wherever they could find it and then finally order Isoline some new dresses from a seamstress Bess was familiar with. Bellamira had been too out of sorts to discuss the financial matter of the clothes with Isoline, so Bess coordinated the discussion with Bellamira's maid, thus saving Isoline from having to speak about money directly.

It had been so long since Isoline had ridden in a carriage, she had nearly forgotten about the horrible accident until the horses pulling her aunt's black carriage stopped in front of her as she waited on the stoop.

Immediately, her heart started to race and she squeezed poor Bess's hand until it was white.

"Miss Isoline?" Bess asked gently. "Are you all right? I have some smelling salts."

Isoline nearly laughed, which helped calm her down. She had never considered herself to be the sort who needed to carry such a thing, but Bess was ready for any situation. She loosened her grip on Bess's hand but did not let her go.

"I...simply recalled that horrible accident I was in," she said, shaking her head. "But I am glad you are here with me."

Bess smiled and patted Isoline's hand. "Whatever you need, miss," she said. "We are all here for you."

Isoline nodded, took a deep breath, and climbed into the carriage with Bess by her side.

They arrived at the church without incident, and Isoline was thrilled to be able to take in more of the countryside as they traveled. The road occasionally trailed close enough to the ocean they could see the waves, but usually they were surrounded on both sides with bright grass and tall trees. They passed several smaller estates and acres and acres of farmland. Cows and sheep and horses all watched with a distinct lack of interest as they rode by. The closer to town they got, the smaller the houses became and they appeared more often. Isoline was thrilled to see more people on the journey than she had seen in the months since her arrival at Thornrush. She didn't realize just how much she craved human companionship. She decided that any amount of theological posturing she had to feint for a few minutes of cordial discussion with other parishioners before and after the sermon would be worth it.

The churchyard was already crowded with people when she arrived. She saw the vicar along with several other men and women overseeing a dozen children who were getting their energy out before having to sit for the hour-long sermon. As soon as he saw her, he gave her a small wave, and then motioned to the woman next to him. They both came over to greet Isoline before her feet even touched the ground.

"I am so glad to see you have made it," he said as he shook her hand with a warm smile.

"As am I," she replied. "This is my maid, Bess."

"Yes, of course," the vicar said, shaking Bess's hand as well. He then presented his wife, placing his hand on her back as he introduced her. "This is my longsuffering wife, Beatrice."

She took Isoline's hand in hers in a warm grasp not unlike her husband's. "I am so sorry I was not able to meet you yesterday," she said. "My husband had nothing but nice things to say of you."

"And he of you," Isoline said. "And he made me feel so welcome, I simply had to come today."

"Well, we are thrilled to have a new member of the community," she said.

"Oww!" one of the children shrieked. "If you touch me again, I'll..."

"Excuse me!" Beatrice said as she rushed off to mediate an ensuing battle.

Isoline and the vicar chuckled.

"How many of the children are yours?" she asked.

"Oh, only three," he said. "The boy there, and the twin girls."

The boy appeared to be about five and the girls only three. The little family reminded Isoline of her own, which brought a small pang of sadness. She missed her brothers and was sad she was not there for Eunice. She would have to write to them all as soon as she returned home.

"Let us head inside," the vicar said. "We should begin soon."

Isoline nodded, and she and Bess took seats in a middle pew. Other people, men and woman, gave polite nods, but did not introduce themselves. Just before the sermon began, she saw Tristan enter the building. He gave her a large smile and wave. She gave him a demure smile and finger wave back and then turned her attention to the vicar.

The sermon passed quickly, though Isoline couldn't remember much of it afterward. She was too preoccupied with taking in all the new faces and observing the style of clothes the ladies wore. If she was going to get some new frocks, she wanted make sure to choose some that the other women could have no qualms with.

As everyone stood to leave, Isoline took her time heading out. She was in no rush and wanted to make herself available should anyone want to make introductions. She stood in line and waited patiently to thank the vicar and his wife for their service.

"That's her niece, so I've heard," she heard a woman behind her say, but she did not turn her hear.

"The Payne dynasty ended the day the last earl married that woman," another woman said.

"Shame," the first woman said. "Thornrush Manor should stand as a beacon for the community, not a mausoleum to one old woman. What can she possibly do up there by herself all day?"

"Count her money and stare down on the rest of us," the second woman said, and the two tittered between them.

Isoline pursed her lips and bit her tongue. It was horrible, the things the women were saying of her aunt, but she didn't want to make a scene or enemies on her first day in town.

"Do you think there's any truth in what they say?" a third woman who had apparently been listening to the conversation as well piped up. "About her having a hand in the death of Lord Granville?"

Isoline's heart froze. How could they so causally accuse her aunt of murdering her husband?

"Probably," one of the other women—Isoline had lost track of who was saying what—said. "She never remarried though. What's the point of doing one husband in if you don't have another one waiting in the wings?"

The three laughed as though they shared a great joke.

"Miss Beresford!" the vicar said, breaking into Isoline's thoughts. She had been so busy eavesdropping on the vile conversation behind her, she hadn't realized she was now at the front of the line. "I do hope you enjoyed yourself."

Isoline forced a smile to her face. "Of course," she said. "Very inspirational."

"I am afraid we already have plans for supper today," he said. "But perhaps next week you could join us for a meal afterward."

She looked at the kind and earnest faces of the vicar and his wife and nodded. She couldn't let the gossip of a few biddies ruin the wonderful day she'd had so far and stop her from enjoying time with the new friends she had made.

"I look forward to it," Isoline said.

As she exited the church and stood in the sun, she took a deep breath to calm herself and clear her mind.

"Cousin Isoline!" Tristan called out. He must have been waiting for her to exit the church because he was instantly by her side.

"Oh!" she said, surprised. "How nice to see you again, Tristan."

"May I walk you to your carriage?" he asked, holding out his hand.

She nodded and placed her hand in his. She immediately felt eyes on her as several church members watched Tristan escort her across the yard. She felt her stomach drop. She was certain that everyone would suddenly think Tristan was courting her, and she had no way to squash such an assumption. She would have to clarify things with the vicar the next weekend when they ate together.

"I am so glad to see you here today," Tristan said. "I have missed your company."

"We are friends," Isoline said. "You needn't fear making a social call occasionally." She almost immediately regretted her words as Tristan's eyes lit up.

"I will do that," he said. "How about tomorrow? I will see you then, dear cousin!" He didn't wait for her response before he kissed the back of her hand and then verily skipped back across the yard to stand with a few other gentlemen who no doubt who congratulate him on his "fine catch."

She shook her head and nearly felt sick as she climbed into the carriage.

"Are you all right, miss?" Bess asked. "You seemed to have turned a bit green."

"No," Isoline said. "I'm not all right." She shook her head and again and dropped it into her hand, about to cry.

"Mrs. Yardly," Bess said. "Her husband is having an affair with a viscount's wife in York. Everyone knows it." Isoline looked up at her confused, but Bess continued. "And Lady Winchester, she can't have a child of her own. She's right bitter about it. You should hear the things she said when the vicar's wife came home with twins. Venom she was spitting."

"Who are you...?" Isoline started to ask, but Bess predicted her question.

"The women behind us who were speaking ill of Lady Granville," she said. "Miserable, the lot of them. So they don't have anything nice to say about anyone. Makes them feel superior."

Isoline reached over and squeezed Bess's hand. She gave her a small smile and wiped the dampness from the edges of her eyes.

"Don't fret over old rumors, miss," Bess continued. "The countess has long stopped giving them a second thought."

"Thank you, Bess," Isoline said.

CHAPTER NINE

The next day, true to his word, Tristan called, bright and early. Isoline had only finished her breakfast and was getting ready for her walk when Talbot announced his arrival.

"Dear Cousin!" Tristan said as he walked over and gripped her hands in his. He continued to hold them as he made his way to the couch, forcing her to sit next to him instead of across. "I am so glad you invited me to call."

"Well, we are family, and friends. It's an open invitation," she said as she pried her fingers loose and motioned to Talbot for tea. She was certain his smile quivered at the word "friend," but she ignored it.

"Did you enjoy the sermon yesterday?" he asked.

She couldn't remember the details but nodded nonetheless. "Of course," she said.

"All that talk about love and eternity," he said. "It certainly makes you think, does it not?"

"*God's* love and *heavenly* eternity are certainly deep thoughts for contemplation," she said, determined not to let the conversation travel in the direction he so clearly wanted it to.

"Yes...yes, of course," he said. "But certainly, it also makes you think about life here and now."

"Not really," Isoline said, exasperated. "I just take life day to day. I'm very happy here, caring for my aunt and spending time with myself. I wouldn't change a thing."

"Spending time with yourself?" he asked with a huff. "Or spending time with a certain vagrant who leeches off of our Aunt Bellamira."

"I don't know what you are talking about," she said, crossing her arm. Had he been spying on her? Watching her? How did he know she had seen Auberon again?

"Don't you?" he asked as he stood and went to the fireplace. He then turned back to her. "I'm only trying to protect you, Isoline."

She stood and took a few steps away, glad of the distance between them. "And I don't recall asking for your protection."

"I suppose I should have left you in the rain, sobbing and drenched," he said.

"If I had known it would lead to this I certainly wish you would have," she snapped back.

"What?" he asked. "Led to me loving you? You ungrateful—"

"Loving me?" she guffawed. "You don't know me. I don't know a thing about you, except that you don't listen. I told you that I was only interested in your friendship."

"Come now, cousin," he said. "We both know that our relationship has developed way beyond that."

"What relationship?" she asked, exasperated. "I can count on one hand how many times we have spoken."

"But if it is love at first sight—" he started, taking a brisk step toward her.

She stepped back, keeping her hands well out of reach. "It's not love!" she exclaimed, startled by the volume of her own voice.

"What is the meaning of this?" Bellamira demanded as she entered the room. "I swear I can hear the two of you bickering all the way up in my rooms. Makes me glad I never had children of my own."

"I am so sorry, aunt," Isoline said rushing to her side. "I never wish to disturb you."

"Nor I, aunt," Tristan said as he smoothed his hair back. "Isoline and I were just having an...impassioned discussion."

"If that is how you discuss things," Bellamira said, "I should hate to know how you fight."

"I would never fight with dear Isoline," Tristan said with a cool grace that only made Isoline more angry. "I simply declared my feelings for her and I think she may have been overcome with emotion."

"I am not emotional," Isoline said, clenching her fists. It was taking all of her energy to keep from screaming once again. "Well, maybe I am upset, but only because you refuse to listen to me. I know what I am saying."

"Declare your emotions?" Bellamira asked, her mouth curled in only what Isoline could describe as disgust. "What is going on here?"

"I'm in love with Isoline," Tristan declared without hesitation. "She is all I think about and I wish to court her with a view to marriage."

"But...but you've only just met," Bellamira said in surprise.

"I have known from the moment I found her in the rain," he said with a sigh. "I know it might not have happened as quickly for her. I accept that. I only ask that she allow me to court her so that in time she may too realize her love for me."

"And you, Isoline?" Bellamira asked. "Are you open to this...this whirlwind courtship your cousin has proposed?"

"No," Isoline said firmly. "I don't want to be courted by anyone. I only ever offered Tristan my friendship and familial affection, nothing more. I came here to be with you auntie, not to find a husband. You will recall that the whole reason I am here is because I called off an engagement. I have no wish to be married."

"So what is the problem?" Bellamira asked, turning back to Tristan. "You proposed a courtship and Isoline said no. What is all the fuss about?"

"B-because..." he stammered, as though shocked Bellamira did not see things his way. "She only needs to give me a chance to earn her love."

"I don't think Isoline would agree," Bellamira said. "Perhaps in time, Isoline might change her mind, but not with you badgering her and stomping around like some sort of bull elephant."

Isoline couldn't help but chuckle at her aunt's description, which was quite spot on, but it seemed to only irritate Tristan further.

"Grand-Auntie," Tristan pleaded. "You must see that I only have Isoline's best interest at heart. If you could only persuade her—"

"Tristan, dear nephew," Bellamira cut in raising her hand to stop him from speaking further. "I will do no such thing. I am not her mother, and even if I were, she is not a child. She is a young woman with her own mind. And if she uses that mind to make a decision, neither you nor I should waste our energy trying to change it. I think you should go."

Tristan's face grew red and he pressed his lips to keep from railing at his aunt. Isoline held her breath, afraid he was not going to take their aunt's words to heart. But finally, he did. He stormed out of the room, and both Isoline and Bellamira waited until they heard the front door close before they exhaled again.

"Oh, auntie," Isoline whimpered as she sunk to the couch.

Bellamira waved her off as she asked Talbot for a fresh pot of tea to calm their nerves. "That boy has always been rather spoiled. Doted on by his mother. So demanding of his father. Both of his sisters married quite young—*too* young—largely I think to get away from him. He has calmed down in recent years, mostly since his parents died and he had to take care of himself. And he has been an amiable companion to me, he helps me keep the accounts, and he visits regularly, but I am not of courting age," she said with a wry chuckle.

Isoline smiled but was unable to find the humor in the situation at the moment. She did wonder why Tristan had spent so much time over the years with Bellamira and not looking for a wife. Surely there were available young ladies in town, or he could have found one in London during the season.

She thought about what Royston, her brother, had said about Bellamira's fortune. That she had never, in all her years, named an heir. Perhaps he was in a similar boat as Isoline, trying to ingratiate himself with the elderly relative in the hopes of securing a fortune. Maybe he saw Isoline as some sort of threat to plans he had been working toward for so long. She didn't think he needed it, though. He had a modest estate of his own. Maybe that wasn't it. Maybe he did love her. She shook her head. She had no way of knowing his true motives and she didn't want to find them out. She just wanted him to leave her alone.

"I am...proud of you, Isoline," Bellamira said as though she knew she shouldn't say it but couldn't help herself.

"Proud?" Isoline asked. "Of what?"

Bellamira sat thoughtfully for a moment before she explained. "When I was a girl, we didn't have a choice in these matters. It wasn't, 'darling, would you like to marry Lord Granville?' It was, 'next month, darling, you are to marry Lord Granville.' I had never even met him before. And he was twice my age! But there was nothing I could do about it. It was expected of me. Of all the girls back then. Of course, we dreamed of love and romance, but we knew it didn't really exist for us."

Isoline nodded sorrowfully. Such marriages without choice were still common. That Isoline's father had allowed her to call off her marriage to Cyril was in many ways a very modern attitude. One many fathers would not tolerate.

"You might think that I had a good life, an easy one when you look at this large house and beautiful pieces of art," Bellamira went on. "But believe me, my girl, I paid for them in their own way. Every last one of them."

Bellamira's face had grown hard, defiant, angry, yet there was hurt behind her eyes. Isoline had no wish to ask what a young Bellamira had suffered at the hands of her husband, but she did not need to know. Bellamira's face said enough. Lord Granville had been a cruel man. After enduring such a marriage, it was no surprise that Bellamira never remarried. She had probably had more than enough of men after that.

"I'm proud of you, my darling," Bellamira said, "because

you knew marrying that little lord was the wrong decision. You stood up for yourself and said damn to the consequences. You had no idea I would open my home to you. You could have ended up in a nunnery, or worse, but you didn't give in. And just now, with Tristan, it would be a good match. If you father knew about the offer, he would be quite glad of it, I'm sure. But no. You stayed firm in your resolve. You were very brave."

Bellamira's gushing adoration nearly brought tears to Isoline's eyes again, but not in sadness. She rushed to her aunt's side and gave her a tight hug.

"Thank you, dear auntie," Isoline said.

"Now, there, there," Bellamira said, patting her back and then pushing her away gently. "Enough of that. How about a game of cards before luncheon?"

*B*y mid-afternoon, Bellamira was exhausted, so she went to her apartments to lay down. Isoline never did get to take her daily walk because a summer storm rolled in with thunder and a gentle rain. Isoline decided she should resume her exploration of the house. She could not explain why the similar portraits of her and her grand-aunt had disturbed her so. It was quite common for people who were related to each other to look similar. If anything, she should be honored to look so like her dear auntie.

She went back to the second floor and entered a room she had not been in before. This one appeared to be an office, with a large desk sitting in front of a window and several shelves of books. There were still many pieces of art to be found, but not as many as she had seen in some of the other rooms.

As she examined the art, she actually found several pieces she quite admired. One appeared to be a quite simple rendering of a black horse on a white background in some sort of oriental style. But as she looked closer, she realized that she was not looking at a painting, but an exquisitely detailed piece of embroidery. She knew she had to have it. She also found a painting of a knight kissing his beloved lady as he slipped out a window. It was quite scandalous, but she could not ignore the beauty of the piece and decided to set it aside for herself as well. Another piece she adored was of an elegantly dressed man and woman who appeared to be in animated discussion. "Beatrice and Benedict," the piece was called, and she laughed at the thought of an artist capturing the classic couple as they tossed verbal barbs at each other.

She quickly realized that she was already collecting too many pieces. If she found this many in one room, how many more would she find in the others? She needed to make a list of the ones she liked and where in the house they could be found. Then, when Auberon called, he could help her decide which pieces to move to her room.

She decided she needed some paper and a pencil, and she would make a list of all the rooms and the pieces she favored in each one. As she walked over to the desk, the rain, heavier now, patted on the window. She looked out and thought she saw someone, a man, standing in the rain looking up at her.

She started and looked more closely. Lightning lit up the sky and the thunder crashed, causing her to gasp and step back. When the rumbling cleared, she looked again, but the man was gone, if he had ever been there at all. She shook her head. She must have simply imagined it.

She turned to the desk and opened the top drawer. She pulled out some loose pieces of paper, but most of them already had writing on them. She gasped when one of them crumbled in her hands it was so old. She carefully laid the others down and looked them over to see what they were. The handwriting and words seemed ancient. She could just barely make them out, but they didn't all make sense to her. She finally found a date on one of them. 1756.

1756? That was nearly a hundred years ago! She scanned the page again and realized it was some sort of rental agreement.

The Third Earl of Payne does hearby rent ten acres of land and a cottage in perpetuity to one Auberon Dracoia.

Isoline stood up straight and let the words sink in. A writ of agreement between a long-dead earl and Auberon from 1756? That...that simply couldn't be possible.

A breeze blew, scattering some of the papers Isoline had been looking at. She quickly did her best to gather the pages before they were lost or damaged. She then looked for the source of the breeze. The window she had been looking out just moments ago was now slightly ajar. But she was certain that is had been closed when she last looked out it. She shook her head. It must have been closed but unlatched and the wind blew it free. She closed the window and made sure the latch was tight before she returned to the mysterious writ of deed.

She willed her breath to still and her mind to clear. Certainly, the deed could not have been written for her

Auberon. Well, the Auberon she knew. He certainly wasn't *her* Auberon. It must have been written for his father or grandfather. Perhaps the Dracoia family had been renting the land from the Granvilles for generations. That would certainly explain why Bellamira was loathed to dismiss him from the estate, as Tristan had suggested. She would not want to evict someone whose family had been renting on the land since before she had married into it.

Isoline shook her head at her own silliness and gingerly placed the papers back into the drawer. Of course, the renter had been one of Auberon's ancestors. It made perfect sense.

She decided to look for a notebook in her own room so she wouldn't risk disturbing such ancient records again.

CHAPTER TEN

*T*he next day, the sky was clear and the air was warm. It was just the beginning of autumn, and here in the north, it could already be chilly this time of year. But today was not one of those days. Isoline paced in her room, wondering why Auberon had not yet called on her. She had not been on a walk for days just in case she ended up not being home if he decided to call. But finally, she decided she was not going to sit around and wait for him to grace her with his presence. She was going for a walk, and if he showed up while she was out, he could wait for her.

Among the new items she had ordered while in town with Bess was a new walking dress and comfortable walking shoes, which she was excited to break in. She took a light wrap with her just in case she needed it and donned a hat to shield her from the sun.

She decided to walk in a new direction, straight north of the manor house, specifically in the opposite direction of Auberon's cottage. After only a few steps, she could feel the fresh air filling her lungs and releasing any pent-up anxiety. She could hear birds singing and goats bleating. She walked along a fence line and petted the ponies on the other side. She passed some workers in a field who doffed their hats at her. She was truly starting to love it here, to feel like this was home. In only a few days, she would be having luncheon with the vicar and his family and hopefully making some real friends besides her aunt.

Thoughts of her aunt did give her a bit of concern. Last night at dinner, she once again went to bed soon after, complaining of tiredness. Isoline thought her aunt's face was showing a few more wrinkles than when she had first met her. Her eyes still had a slight fogginess to them and she moved more slowly. Isoline had not said anything because she didn't want to insult her, but she was worried. Even though her aunt had seemed healthy and spry only a couple of months before, for a woman of ninety it would not be surprising for her to suddenly show her age, Isoline supposed. She had not met many—any—people of such an age in her life so she didn't know for sure. But something was wrong, or had at least changed. Isoline had no idea what nor any idea of how to bring it up, if she should at all.

Then, of course, there was the issue of the inheritance. Bellamira had not mentioned her will once, and Isoline could not broach the issue. To even inquire about Bellamira's final wishes could imply that she was interested in a portion of the estate, which could cause Bellamira great offense. All Isoline could do was treat her aunt kindly and hope Bellamira thought well enough of her to leave her something. But she had no way of knowing if Bellamira would do that. She couldn't count on an inheritance being there for her if Bellamira were to die or lose her faculties.

This was why Isoline needed a friend in her life. Someone she could speak with and relieve her burdens. For now, she could only shake her head and focus on putting one foot in front of another as she enjoyed her morning walk.

As she took another deep breath and rededicated herself to her little adventure, she realized she was in a large open glade surrounded by trees. She had been here before. No, that was not possible. She had never been in this direction. But...she knew this place.

It was the glade from her dreams.

She looked left and right, turned in a complete circle. She was sure of it. She had been here a hundred, a thousand times before while she was asleep.

But now, she was awake.

Wasn't she?

Of course she was. She had awoken that morning to the light filtering in through her curtains and the doves cooing on the windowsill. She had gone downstairs for breakfast. She then went back to her room, but was restless. Bess helped her dress and she left the house for her walk, ending up here. It was all clear as day in her mind. Yet, somehow, she had ended up here, in the place from her dreams.

She extended her fingers and touched the tips of the grass. It felt the exact same as in her dreams. The same type of grass, the same length of it. She took a few steps and thought it felt strange, not feeling the wet ground under her feet or the blades of glass tickle her calves.

No, she was certainly awake. She was still wearing her new walking dress. She only ever wore her sleeping garment in her dreams.

Perhaps the glade in her dream was based on this one, this very real place. She always thought it had been only a figment of her imagination, but no. It was this glade. It was real. But how was that possible? She had never been to

Thornrush Manor in her life. How could she dream of a place she had never seen?

Of course, she also dreamed of him, and she had never seen him either. He seemed to know that she would one day come here. He must have created this place in her mind. After all, he also knew that she would be coming to Thornrush to care for her aunt. *All will be well*, he had said. He had known it all along that she would be sent here and that she would end up here, in this very glade.

But...*how?* Who was he? And how was he able to create such images in her mind?

Isoline...

She froze. He was here. *Here.* But she wasn't dreaming. How was it possible for him to be here while she was awake?

"Who are you?" she asked. "W-where are you?"

This wasn't right. He couldn't simply come to life, appear out of her dreams. She then felt him. Felt his presence somewhere in the glade, somewhere nearby. She looked all around but didn't see him.

Isoline...

She cried out as she felt his voice and his breath on her ear. She turned her head, but no one was there.

"Show yourself!" she yelled, but no one appeared. Yet, she could still feel him somewhere nearby. She didn't know why she felt afraid, but she did. He had never hurt her, and she didn't believe he ever would. But this wasn't right. Something was happening, something wrong.

She took off at a run.

Isoline!

She thought she heard him not just say her name, but yell it, and that only spurred her to run quicker toward the edge of the glade. She needed to get back home, back to

Thornrush. She realized that she had gotten turned around in the glade and did not know if she was facing the right direction to return home, but she ran nonetheless. The trees surrounding the glade were getting closer. If she could only get there, he would disappear, she was sure of it.

"Isoline?"

As she reached the tree line, someone stepped in front of her, and she screamed in fright.

"Don't touch me!" she yelled as she broke away from him.

"Isoline? What's wrong?" Auberon asked.

She gasped and looked up. Auberon! It was him.

"A-Auberon," she stammered. "What...who...how..."

"Are you all right?" he asked as he placed a protective hand on her shoulder and looked around the glade. "Is someone chasing you?"

She realized then how silly she would sound if she admitted that she had been startled by elements of her dreams while she was awake. It was all so ridiculous. She couldn't have just had a dream while she was asleep. This wasn't the same glade! She must have just heard the wind in her ear.

She sighed and shook her head in embarrassment. "I think a rabbit or small dear must have startled me," she finally said. "It's nothing. I must look quite a fool."

He gave her a comforting smile, but it didn't quite reach his eyes, which still carried a hint of worry. "Don't worry," he said. "I'll escort you back to the house. I was on my way to see you anyway."

"Really?" Isoline asked, her heart racing with excitement instead of fear. "About time."

"Forgive my delay," he said. "I recently had a surge of inspiration and had to start on a new painting. Sometimes when I feel the urge to create, I lose all sense of the world around me."

"That is quite wonderful," Isoline said. "I wish I could be so impassioned about something I lost track of time."

"I am sure that you will find your passion, dear Isoline," he said.

As he said her name, she feared she had already found it.

As they walked back, she remembered the odd writ of deed she found in the desk in the house.

"Has your family rented that cottage for many years?" she asked.

"My family?" he asked, looking at her curiously.

"Yes," she said. "Your father, grandfather? I found a writ of deed in my aunt's house that was signed by an Auberon Dracoia. Were you named after your grandfather?"

"Oh, that," he said looking ahead, moving a low branch out of their way. "Of course. I had completely forgotten."

"Forgotten?" she asked with a curious chuckle. "How could you forget? It was dated over a hundred years ago."

He gave a small laugh in return. "I meant I forgot where the paperwork was. It's been so long I just take the rental for granted. I suppose I should make sure everything is still legal and up to date in case..."

He paused. Isoline could feel his hesitation. He probably had concerns similar to Isoline's. They both lived here at Thornrush at the pleasure of her aunt. If the estate became the property of the crown after her aunt's death, or went to some unknown heir, they could both find themselves out on their ears. They passed by the same workers she had seen earlier, so she knew they were on the right path back, and nodded at them again. They were another concern. She did not know how many tenant farmers and employees there were at Thornrush, but there were many. What would become of them should something happen to her aunt? That was not an eventuality best left to chance. It was an uncomfortable topic of conversation Isoline would have to brook with her aunt...eventually.

"Is something on your mind, Isoline?" Auberon asked after they walked some distance in silence.

She shook her head. "Nothing to bother you with," she said.

"You are never a bother, Isoline," he said, and they both slowed as they looked at each other. He reached up and barely, gently touched her cheek. His fingers were warm and soft. She started to close her eyes, to absorb his warmth, but she shook her head and took a step away.

"I'm sorry," he said, dropping his hand. "I shouldn't have done that. But your face...You are just so beautiful. I wish to...to learn every line, every freckle. I do wish you would reconsider my offer to paint you."

She laughed and resumed their walk. "Oh, I see," she said. "Always the artist. Only ever thinking of your next masterpiece."

He nodded. "That is true," he said. "I am never more alive than when I am bringing something to life on canvas."

"I would love to see your work sometime," she said as the manor house came into view.

"Of course," he said. "Come to the cottage whenever you like."

She blushed a little. She did not think it would ever be appropriate for her to visit his cottage unchaperoned. Perhaps she could convince Bess to accompany her.

As they approached the house, Talbot opened the door without them having to knock, and Isoline handed him her hat and wrap. The usually unflappable butler seemed to start, though, when he saw Auberon.

"Talbot," Isoline said. "You surely know Mr. Dracoia."

"Yes, yes of course, Mr. Dracoia," he said quickly. "Can I help you, sir?"

Auberon entered the foyer and looked around with his hands folded behind his back. "No, Talbot. Thank you," he said.

"Mr. Dracoia is here to help me evaluate auntie's incredible art collection," Isoline said.

"Indeed," Talbot said, his stoicism returned other than a small quirk of his eyebrow.

"Yes," Isoline said. "Could you have some tea sent to the office on the second floor.

"Of course, miss," Talbot said.

"It has been quite some time since I have been here," Auberon said. "It hasn't changed a bit."

"My aunt does seem to be rather set in her ways, in many respects," Isoline said. "Would you care to see which pieces have already caught my eye?" She started to head up the stairs.

"I'd love to—" he started to say but was interrupted by a shriek from the top of the stairs.

"Traitor!" Bellamira yelled down at them. She was holding a paper in her hand and stared down at Isoline with fury in her eyes.

"Aunt?" Isoline asked. "What's wrong?"

"What's wrong?" Bellamira asked as she gripped her gown and held it tightly as she descended the stairs. "This! This is what's wrong."

"Auntie," Isoline said, trying to calm her down. "We have a guest. You know Mr. Dracoia."

"I *know* Mr. Dracoia," Bellamira snapped. "Or do you think I've completely lost my faculties as well?"

"What are you talking about, auntie?" Isoline asked.

"This!" Bellamira said as she thrust the paper at Isoline.

Isoline took it, uncrumpling the page from Bellamira's furious grip. It was the society page, ripped from the local weekly lady's journal. Isoline was unaware the community even *had* a local lady's journal. She had never seen it among the mail. As far as she knew, they only received the *Herald* and the *Lady's Newspaper*, both from London and a day late since they lived so far away.

But Isoline immediately located the section that had infuriated her so.

The niece and presumptive heir of The Dowager Countess of Payne, Lady Bellamira Granville, finally made her long-awaited debut to the community. Miss Isoline Beresford, twenty-two and unmarried, was seen at the local church followed by luncheon at the Rock and Eagle public house. Miss Beresford was overheard remarking on the poor health of her aunt before buying several new dresses from The Well-Dressed Lady boutique. It is the prediction of this columnist that despite Miss Beresford's age, she will soon be the most eligible heiress in the county.

"This...this is preposterous!" Isoline exclaimed, her hands nearly shaking as she read the paper. "Is this what qualifies as news in this backwater community?"

"Is this why you are here?" Bellamira spat. "Just waiting for me to die so you can take my place as Lady of the Manor?"

"No!" Isoline said sincerely. "I am here because I want to be with my aunt. I love it here, and I love spending time with you. I...I don't believe I said anything about your health. You are the healthiest woman I know, regardless of age."

"Well, whether you intended it or not," her aunt said, regaining her composure but not losing any of her anger, "the whole county now thinks I'm going to keel over any moment. And luncheon in a *public house?* Have you no sense of decency?"

Isoline's jaw dropped. "What...what were we supposed to eat? Were we to starve until we came home?"

"Yes!" her aunt cried, exasperated. "Really, Isoline. I cannot begin to express my disappointment." She shook her head and turned to go back up the stairs.

"I'm so sorry, aunt," Isoline called behind her, but Bellamira did not acknowledge her. After she was out of sight, Isoline sighed and shook her head.

"I suppose examining Bellamira's art collection is off the table now," Auberon said with surprising levity.

Isoline's head shot up. She had forgotten he was still there. "Mr. Dracoia," she said. "I am so sorry about that. I don't know what happened."

"Think nothing of it," he said with a smile as he headed toward the door. "Lady Granville has always been a... passionate woman. I'm sure she will calm down soon and all will be well."

Her heart froze. *All will be well*. That was the same thing the man in her dreams had told her. Of course, it was a common enough phrase, and Auberon was only trying to quell her fears. She was just on edge from her experience in the glade, and now with her aunt's outburst...

"I...I hope so," she finally said, escorting Auberon to the door.

"Just wait a few days," he said. "I will call on you again.

Until later, dear Isoline." He took her hand in his and gently kissed the back of it, reviving the butterflies who had not risen there since she last saw him. He smiled as he walked down the front steps. She watched him walk away until he rounded the corner of the house, then she finally, slowly, closed the door.

As she climbed the stairs to her room, she felt surprisingly calm and content, despite the fact that her aunt might throw her out at any moment.

CHAPTER ELEVEN

My Dear Eunice,

I hope all is well. How are you feeling? Can you ask Father if I may come for a visit as soon as the baby arrives? I miss all of you so very much.

Life here is very quiet. I have plenty of time for myself and my thoughts, but not much with which to occupy my time or my mind. I try to enjoy a brisk walk every day, but storms that roll in from the ocean often thwart my plans. Aunt Bellamira has an incredible art collection, one that would put any museum to shame, so I spend quite a bit of time admiring each piece. But how I do wish I had more to do. Listen to me complaining when you probably have more than you can handle in preparation for the newest Beresford. How I wish I could be there to help you. If there is anything I could do for you from so far away, please let me know.

My thoughts are with you all ways,

Your devoted sister,

Isoline

*I*soline looked at the pathetic letter before her and considered crumpling it up and tossing it into the rubbish bin. Her life was so boring and lonely she could not even invent anything interesting to say.

For fear of upsetting Bellamira, or of someone to use the trip against her, she had not gone to church that day and had sent her excuses to the vicar and his wife for missing luncheon with them. Not that Bellamira had noted her presence. She had taken all of her meals in her rooms for the past two days.

Isoline heard a bit of thunder rumble in the distance, and her curtains fluttered from a little stream of wind that came in the room through a crack in the window. She did not rush to close it. The wind was not cold, but clean and refreshing. Out of habit, she pulled her robe more tightly around herself as she took one last look at the sad epistolary before her and then shook her head before placing it into a drawer of the desk, never to be seen again. She wanted write to her family, Eunice in particular, but until she had something more interesting to say, she would not.

She stood and walked over to the window. As she looked out into the yard, she wondered what had brought her to this sorry state. No, she no longer blamed herself, or the man in her dream, for breaking off her engagement and coming to Thornrush Manor. She had done the right thing. She could never have married Cyril. Or, if she had, she would only have been miserable. No, she was glad she had ended things with him. In fact, for the few months before that cursed newspaper article, she had been something nearing on happy. Oh, life had not been perfect. She was bored, and she was displeased with the way things had ended with Tristan. In his own words, they were cousins!

Could he not accept her only as a friend and family member? In spite of that, she was enjoying her life here and getting to know her grand-auntie. She had been on the cusp of making friends in town. And, even though she knew she should not, she was enjoying Auberon's company. She had not known if her aunt would leave her an inheritance, but she wasn't overly concerned with that. Bellamira had seemed healthy and mentally strong and not keen on dying anytime soon. Isoline had simply been enjoying day to day life and wanted for little.

But all that changed with the arrival of the clipping from the lady's weekly.

In one fell swoop, whoever had *anonymously* penned that salacious article had thrown her whole life into chaos and uncertainly. As had whoever then chose to cut it out and send it to Bellamira. It had certainly been a deliberate act. Isoline had searched the house from top to bottom and, as she had suspected, she did not find a single issue of the local lady's journal. She asked Talbot about it, and he told her that Bellamira specifically did not subscribe to the journal because she didn't want to be involved in whatever cat fights or chicken cluckings the ladies of the village were reveling in. Whoever sent the article must have known this, which was why they sent it. To be sure that Bellamira would see it.

But who would do such a thing? The only thing to be gained from it would be to create a rift between Isoline and Bellamira. There was only one person who would want to do that—her "dear cousin" Tristan. She had asked Talbot directly if he knew who had sent the note, but he said it had been unsigned, which she believed. No one would be foolish enough to leave a direct trail to the culprit. Besides, after Bellamira had so unceremoniously dismissed Tristan from her home the last time they had seen him, surely she wouldn't put any credence into anything he had to say.

But he didn't say it. He didn't need to. Even if Bellamira ignored him, she couldn't ignore what had been written in the newspaper. But who had written the article? Certainly not Tristan. Even though some men did write articles for ladies' magazines, and most editors and owners of such journals were always men, the society pages were strictly the realm of women. It would be beneath a man to write about such things, especially a man such as Tristan. No, he didn't write it. But he saw it well enough, and saw his chance to drive a wedge between his aunt and his cousin and sent it off to Bellamira immediately. The author probably didn't know the extent of the damage she would do. It was most likely one of those gossiping women who had been behind her at church. They intentionally wrote it to make Isoline look like a scheming treasure hunter and drudge up old rumors about Bellamira in the minds of the locals. It was unlikely they had any idea that their words would cause strife between Isoline and Bellamira.

Well, their intentions didn't matter. The damage had been done, and Isoline now lived each day on uncertain and shaky ground. Every time she heard a door open somewhere in the house she thought Bellamira was coming to announce her dismissal.

There was a light tap on her door.

"Come in," Isoline said.

Bess entered the room with a cup of tea and some biscuits. "I thought you might like a spot of tea, miss," she said. "Chamomile. It will help you sleep."

"Thank you, Bess," Isoline said. "How thoughtful."

"Think nothing of it, miss," Bess said. "You just seemed rather on edge today and figured you needed it."

Isoline nodded. "I appreciate it, Bess," she said with a smile, and Bess turned to leave the room. "Bess..." Isoline called out. Bess turned back expectantly. Isoline wanted to ask her if she knew of Bellamira's plans. If she had heard anything. If had any inkling about whether she was to be turned out at dawn. But then she thought better of it. It was a poor mistress who involved her maid in the personal matters of the family. "I...just wanted to apologize for not going to church today and taking you with me. You seemed to enjoy it so much last week. I'm sorry."

Bess waved her off. "I'm quite used to staying here at the house for months on end. No worries, miss."

Isoline nodded, and Bess gave a small curtsey as she left the room. Not for the first time, Isoline wondered how old Bess was. She seemed young, younger that Isoline, but she spoke as if she had served at the house for many years. Of course, it would be rude for Isoline to directly ask Bess how old she was, but maybe she could ask someone else. James or Talbot. Surely she could inquire discreetly.

With her tea already gone, Isoline placed her teacup back on the tray and climbed into bed. It was still early, not even ten o'clock, but there was nothing to keep her awake. The sooner she fell asleep, the sooner tomorrow would come.

But sleep did not come easily. She turned this way and that, falling just to edge of sleep and then waking up again. She began to feel irritated, frustrated. There were too many questions swirling around in her head. Too much uncertainly. She was about to get up when she heard him call her name.

Isoline...

She was certain she had not fallen asleep. She sat up and saw that she was still in her bed, in her room. She looked to the window and saw the curtains fluttering. She started to get up, to go close the window, but she felt his hand on her shoulder.

*Stay...*he said.

She gasped at his touch. His *touch*. For so long he had been unable to actually touch her. He was always just beyond her skin. But now, she could clearly feel his fingers on the soft skin of her upper back. The warmth in his hand. The tiny ridges of his fingertips.

She sat back in the bed and turned to him. In the dark, she still could not see his face, but she was facing him! For the first time, when she turned to him, he was still there.

"How...how is this possible?" she asked.

He reached up and placed a finger to her lips. *Shh...*he said, and she nodded. He then caressed her cheek and ran a finger over her chin. Around her chin. Down her neck. Over her décolletage.

She shuddered and shrunk back. This was wrong. She couldn't allow a man, even him, into her room. Her *bed*. She needed to protect her virtue. Her reputation.

Then she nearly laughed at the absurdity of it. It was only a dream. A dream she had not dared to dream before, but one she had imagined countless times. If she did allow herself a moment of fantasy, of passion, who was to know? Was there a woman alive who had not done the same in her private chambers?

She leaned forward, toward the dark outline of his shape. "Touch me," she whispered.

Once again, he ran his fingers over her cheek, her neck, her chest, just along the edge of her nightgown. This time, she exhaled and shuddered, but she did not pull away. He reached up behind her head and pulled her to him. Gently he placed his lips on hers. They were soft and warm and sent a small shockwave through her body down to the tip of her spine.

She leaned in and kissed him back, urging him on, letting him know that he didn't have to hold back. It was only a dream, after all. Here, she could let her desires run wild.

They both opened their mouths, teasing, nipping, tasting, sucking. It was not her first kiss, but she wondered if she could even count the innocent pecks on her lips Cyril had given her as kisses. They certainly never ignited anything in her like the kisses from this man who before now had only walked at a distance in her dreams.

She wondered what had changed. What had brought him to her now, so fully, so completely. So real. She didn't know. Did she care?

She leaned back on her pillow and pulled him to her. He laid half on top of her, half by her side. He kissed from her mouth, to her cheek, to her neck. He lingered there, breathing in her scent. Licking her skin. Giving her small bites. She gasped and opened her mouth to warn him not to leave any marks her maid might see, but then she remembered that this was only a dream. She felt a tingling ache between her legs and pulled him tighter, closer. She dared to allow herself to moan as his hands explored her body, squeezing her breast through her nightdress. She fumbled at the tie at her neck, loosening it and pulling her collar down, exposing her chest to him. He let out a groan of satisfaction as he worked his way to one nipple, taking it in his mouth and flicking it with his tongue, and then other one.

She arched her back and her eyes rolled back in her head as the tingling pain between her legs turned to a warm, wet need. All thoughts of Cyril, of Tristan, even of Auberon fled her mind. She loved this man. This man she had known for so long. This man who never abandoned her or betrayed her. This man who thrilled her to the core as no other could.

She pulled his face back to hers and opened her legs to him, inviting him to settle between them. She still could not see his face clearly as his dark hair fell, blocking any light from the moon trying to seep into the room. The thunder still grumbled in the distance and rain pelted the window. The wind picked up, throwing the curtain about violently. But she didn't care.

"Say it," she begged.

*Isoline...*he whispered, and she nearly reached the precipice of pleasure at the familiar sound. She took his hand and used it to raise her gown up her thighs.

"Take me," she said, and she felt the weight of him on her body.

He kissed her cheek, her jawline, and moved to her neck. He was taking his time, teasing her, pleasuring her, and she quivered in anticipation.

"Now, please," she said.

Isoline...

"Yes...yes!" she panted.

Then she screamed out as she felt him bite into her neck with such a force she thought he must have drawn blood. Then she groaned as the pain melted away and the most exquisite pleasure coursed through her body. Her body convulsed of its own volition as he continued to bite and suck her neck. She fell onto her pillow and sighed in satisfaction, but satisfaction from what, she wasn't sure. She had never been with a man before, but she was certain that she should not have achieved her pleasure from a bite to the neck.

A bite to the neck, how odd! she thought as her senses

returned to her. She turned to him and he slid away from her and stood up from the bed.

"Wait," she called as she reached out to him.

At that, a clap of thunder sounded, causing her to shrink back and close her eyes. When she reopened them, he was gone.

She flew from her bed and looked out the window. In the yard, she saw him walking away in the rain. She tried to open the window fully so she could call out to him, but it was shut and locked! How was that possible? She knew she had left it open.

She went to her side table and lit a candle. She then returned to the window and worked the clasp free. When she was finally able to throw the window open, there was no one in the yard.

She collapsed in the chair in front of her vanity and shook her head. What had just happened? Had it all been a dream? Or something more? Was she still sleeping now? She was so confused. She looked at herself in the mirror and laughed at the disheveled state of her hair. As she pulled it aside, she saw two puncture marks in her neck and she gasped.

She reached up to touch them, but she felt nothing. Her skin was perfectly smooth. She ran to her wash basin and dipped a cloth into the water, then ran it over her neck. She went back to the mirror and sighed when she saw that the marks were gone. She slumped back into the chair. She must have simply imagined something was there a moment ago. Her mind was spinning, swimming with thoughts of him and what they had just done. If they had done anything.

It had only been a dream...right?

PART III

———————

I do not know whether I was then a man
dreaming I was a butterfly, or whether I am
now a butterfly dreaming I am a man.

~ Zhuangzi

CHAPTER TWELVE

For the next several nights, he did not return. Yet, she did not feel sad about it, which surprised her. Strangely, even though nothing had changed, she did not feel anxious. She realized that, as of now, everything was out of her hands. She could only wait to see what Bellamira would do. She could only wait to see if he returned to her. She could only control herself, not the world around her. She wasn't sure what brought on this new sense of contentment and calm, but she was glad to feel it.

She was having her breakfast in the dining room when Bellamira made an appearance. She stood to greet her aunt.

"Aunt Bellamira!" she called out, nearly dropping her toast and spilling her tea. "I am so happy to see you downstairs, and so early at that."

Bellamira simply waved her off as she sat down and allowed James to prepare a small plate for her. "I realized that I was only still eating breakfast in my room out of habit. It has been only me living here for decades. Why should I eat alone when I finally have a...a guest," she said.

Isoline wasn't sure how to take her aunt's words. Was she being kind by deciding to eat with her? Or was she giving her a warning by calling her merely a "guest?" Isoline wasn't sure, but she couldn't simply ask her aunt directly. She gave a small smile and nod as she sat back down, glad that Bellamira had decided to acknowledge her presence at all.

As they ate, Isoline couldn't help but notice that Bellamira's hands were shaking slightly as she buttered her bread and cut into her sausage. She said nothing, but was concerned. She looked at the woman's face, her hands, the way she moved. She still looked nothing like the ninety-year-old she was, but she had aged probably ten years from when Isoline had first met her.

"I received a note from Auberon," Bellamira said. "He says the frame is done. Do you think you could go to his cottage and fetch it for me?"

Isoline nearly choked on her tea at the mention of Auberon. She had not given him much thought since the night she had spent with the man in her dreams. But at hearing his name, some familiar feelings came fluttering back. Still, she nodded and said she would, as was only proper, glad her aunt was trusting her with the task.

That afternoon, there was a chill on the air. They were well into autumn, so the days of warmth were most likely firmly behind them. Still, a quick walk easily warmed Isoline enough she could loosen her scarf and remove her gloves as she headed toward the cottage.

When she crested the hill, she was both surprised and not surprised to see Auberon standing in front of his cottage admiring the view. She couldn't help but shake her head and smile. No wonder he wasn't married. Was he even capable of looking at a woman the way he looked at that view?

"Waiting for inspiration to strike?" she asked as she approached.

He turned and smiled at her. "I think it just arrived," he said, and her heart leaped.

She sighed to herself in frustration. What was wrong with her? When she was asleep, she clearly was in love with the man in her dreams. But as soon as she found herself in Auberon's presence, she started imagining another life, a real one, one with a very real man.

She needed to make a choice eventually. She would have to decide if the man in her dreams was enough for her or not. But hadn't she already made that choice? Didn't she choose the man in her dreams the day she broke off her engagement? She had made it clear to Bellamira that she wasn't interested in marriage or courtship. And she had meant it. She could have been perfectly happy with just having a man waiting for her to fall asleep if she had never met Auberon. Why did he have to be here? Of all places? Hundreds of miles from where she had grown up. What were the chances that the one man who could shake her resolve would be here?

"Flattery will get you nowhere, Mr. Dracoia," she finally said, and he smirked.

"So, to what do I owe your esteemed presence?" he asked.

"My aunt said you had completed the frame for the painting of the hideous beast," she said. "She instructed me to fetch it for her."

He laughed, deep and throaty from his gullet. "You truly do hate it, don't you?"

"I cannot put into words my disdain for the thing," she said, making a face at just the thought of it.

"What do you know of it?" he asked. "The artist? The story behind it?" Isoline shook her head, since she knew nothing. He smiled and held out his hand. "Please, come with me," he said. "I want to introduce you properly."

She didn't hesitate to take his hand as he led her toward the cottage. He opened the door, and there the painting sat, in the middle of the room on an easel, sitting inside a large gilded frame.

The rest of the room was quite simply furnished, with only a table and chair for dining, a large fireplace with a pot of something stewing that smelled delicious, a cupboard for plates and bowls, and a door leading to the rest of the house.

"Forgive me," he said, apparently able to read her mind as she looked around the room—anywhere but at the painting of the beast. "I know my home is nothing compared to the opulence of Thornrush Manor."

She waved him off. "Think nothing of it," she said. "There is beauty in simplicity."

He nodded. "Quite right. But will you dare to see beauty in the painting before you?"

She forced herself to look at the painting, the demon hunched over the woman. Her hand immediately went to her neck as she thought about the night of passion she shared with the man in her dreams and he had bitten into her neck. Is that what the monster in the painting was about to do to the woman? The very idea made her nauseous.

She shook her head. "I cannot..." She wanted to explain further, but she could not find the words. She moved away and turned her head so she didn't have to look directly at it.

"The painting is called, in my language, 'Ce Vise Pot Veni,'" he said. "Or in English, 'What Dreams May Come.'"

Her breath nearly hitched in her throat at the mention of dreams. "As in...from Shakespeare?" she asked.

"You will find that Shakespeare has nearly universal appeal," he explained.

She nodded. Of course he did. Wasn't that why he was so beloved? Rich or poor, man or woman, British or foreigner. Everyone could relate to at least one of his characters.

"In your language?" Isoline asked. "My aunt said this painting came from Romania. Is that where you, your family, are from?"

"Yes!" he said, excited. "You have heard of it?"

"Only in passing, occasionally in books," she said. "But I would not pretend I know anything of it."

"Yes, I miss it very much," he said.

"You have been there?" Isoline asked.

"I was born there," he said.

"Hmm," Isoline mused. "But your grandfather, he was already renting the land here, you said."

He shrugged. "Family is complicated, no?"

She couldn't help but nod. That was certainly true. "So, the painting," she said, returning to the image that loomed before her. "It is of a dream?"

"It is both of a woman having a dream and the dream itself," he explained. He gently placed his hands on her shoulders and turned her so she had to face the painting squarely. "You see how the woman is sleeping? But in her mind, the man—the monster you see—he is just as real as he is there, sitting on her chest."

She exhaled sharply and shuddered. It was suddenly so clear to her. It was as though the artist had painted her very life. "Why...why do you think he painted this?" she dared to ask.

"The artist, Iasi Busila, said that his wife, the love of his life, had fantastical dreams all of her life," he said, causing Isoline's heart to race. "She often wrote about the dreams when she awoke. Eventually, he started painting what she was writing. He hoped that by bringing the dreams out of her mind and into the real world, they would stop tormenting her."

"And did it work?" she asked. "Did the dreams stop?"

"We don't know," he said. "They lived a long time ago. There have been many wars, much migration, people fleeing, coming back. He and his family were lost to time. But the paintings, they remained in many homes of the aristocracy. That is where Miss Ezerbet found this piece, in the home of a great lord."

She looked back at the painting and suddenly found it far less frightening than before. If anything, it seemed all too familiar, which created a different sort of discomfort, but at least her fear had dissipated.

"You seem very interested in the dream aspect of the painting," Auberon said, as usual, seemingly able to get right to the matter closest to her heard.

She nodded. "I...I think I know something of how Busila's wife must have felt," she admitted. "I too have had very... vivid dreams of late."

"Will you share them with me?" he asked.

She shook her head. "I cannot," she said. "Not yet. Maybe someday."

He chuckled. "They must be very special dreams indeed," he said.

"What do you think?" she asked, trying to redirect the conversation away from her and motioning back to the painting. "Do you give any credence to the idea that our dreams and our awake lives may not be so different?"

He crossed his arms and looked at the painting thoughtfully. "I think Descartes said it best when he said, 'I perceive so clearly that there exist no certain marks by which the state of waking can ever be distinguished from sleep.'"

"Yes!" she said, nearly jumping up and down with excitement. In all her years she had never met a man who knew to what she was referring when she spoke of dreams. "Do we dream only when we sleep? Are we dreaming now? Who can know?"

"The world is a mysterious place," Auberon said. "I cannot begin to understand it, much less explain it."

"But isn't it fun to discuss?" Isoline asked. "To try and see beyond what merely our eyes tell us but the secrets of the mind?"

"Perhaps one day you will tell me your dreams," Auberon said. "Then we can try to understand the mysteries of the universe together."

"I would like that," she said, and she looked back at the painting and realized she was no longer afraid of it, but found a familiar comfort. "Thank you for explaining the painting to me," she said. "You have changed my perception. Truly."

"It was my pleasure to share my knowledge with you," he said.

"Will you show me some of your pieces?" she asked

playfully, pulling him toward the door to the rest of the house.

"Oh, I don't think so," he said with a chuckle. "They cannot compare to a great master like Busila."

"Well, how will I know if I don't have anything to compare to it," she asked as she threw open the door. She looked into the other room and froze. Not for the first time, she saw herself staring back at her.

"I...I didn't want you to see it until it was finished," Auberon said as he rushed to cover the painting with a cloth, but she moved next to him and stilled his hand. She looked at the painting, into the eyes of the girl standing back at her, and nearly wept for the beauty of it.

It was her, truly. It was not a younger version of her aunt. Not her from several years ago when she was merely a girl. But the real her, here and now. But mostly her eyes. In the eyes of the painting, she saw all her own cares and worries, her hopes and desires, and, yes, her dreams. She had never considered herself to be a great beauty. Attractive, certainly. But not exquisite. Not someone anyone would want to paint, to preserve for all eternity. Yet she could not deny that the woman she was looking at was both her and beautiful. Her eyes were dark and large, her skin a pale pink. Her dark hair fell in tendrils around bare shoulders and she wore a dress with a dark red bodice.

"You...you painted this?" she asked, bewildered.

"Well you could certainly say I tried," he said with true humility. "Trying to paint from memory is not the same as having a sitting subject, but I was doing my best."

"This is how you see me in your mind?" she asked.

"Not exactly," he said. "What I see when I close my eyes is only a pale imitation of the woman who is standing here now."

At that, her heart began to sing. It didn't matter whether or not she saw herself or the painting as beautiful. What mattered was that Auberon did. And she could tell that his feelings for her went far beyond her superficial looks. He felt something for her, something deep, something strong for him to have put such effort into his rendition of her. She could no longer deny it, force it to hide deep inside of her. She was falling in love with Auberon, and she believed he felt the same even though neither of them could admit it. Not yet.

"Thank you," she finally whispered. "I love it. What will you do with it when it is complete?"

"I don't know," he admitted. "I hadn't thought that far ahead."

"I think I should love for my Aunt Bellamira to have it," she said. "She has an older painting of me, but not one made with such skill. It would be wonderful to add to her collection. I could buy it from you, of course."

He waved away her offer. "I could never accept money from you. I never accept money for any of my work. Lady Payne allows me to live here for free. I have no real use for money."

Isoline raised an eyebrow. What a charmed life, to have no worry of money. "Still, I couldn't just take such a magnificent piece of art from you. I must compensate you in some way."

He took his hand in hers and brought it to his lips. "You have already given me enough, darling Isoline."

*I*soline laid in bed and replayed the day in her mind. She had brought the framed painting of the woman and the beast back to her aunt, who was ecstatic to finally have it ready to hang on a wall. Now that Isoline no longer feared the thing, she was able to help her aunt find the best place for it. Somewhere it would be seen but not overpower the room. They had agreed to hang it in the parlor, but off to the side. A place where it would be seen by visitors but not distract from meaningful discussion.

That evening, Isoline and Bellamira had played cards until dinner. After which, Bellamira retired to her own quarters and Isoline to hers. Isoline tried again at writing a letter to Eunice, but she found herself too excited to concentrate. Isoline told Auberon that she would return to the cottage every day and sit for the painting until it was finished. Afterward, he would frame it and deliver it to Bellamira himself and present it as a gift. The thought of seeing Auberon the next day, and every day after that, thrilled her to the core. She could hardly wait to sleep and bring the next day forth more quickly.

Yet, she knew that if she were to dream while she slept, he might return. Would he know that she was falling in love with someone else? What would he think? Would he be angry? Would her feelings for Auberon suddenly change if she felt herself in his arms again? She didn't think so. What she was feeling for Auberon was above and beyond anything she had ever felt for a living man before. Stronger than she had felt for the man in her dreams, she was sure. If the man in her dreams was to disappear and never return, she would be satisfied with that. But if Auberon could no longer be in her life, she would be devastated.

She knew she had to face the man in her dreams. She

had to get it over with. She finally forced herself to lie down and sleep. She tossed and turned for many hours, but eventually, sleep claimed her.

He did not make an appearance.

In the morning, she woke refreshed. It had been nearly a week since their passionate encounter and he had returned. Isoline was not distraught by this fact. Instead, she was glad of it. He was not trying to stop her from living her life, from finding love among the living. She took his disappearance as tacit approval of her newfound love for Auberon.

She only needed to know for sure if Auberon felt the same way.

*W*hen she left the house that morning, she only told her aunt she was going for her morning walk. She did not see a reason to worry her over her unchaperoned visit to Auberon's cottage until she knew whether or not her aunt needed to concern herself. Even though she was rather certain that Auberon did not merely see her as an art subject, she needed to ask him directly. She did not want any ambiguity between them. She was in love with him, and she needed to know if he felt the same way before she began to tackle larger issues such as whether her father would ever approve.

When she arrived at the cottage, she was surprised to see that he had set up the easel outside, along with his supplies and a chair for her to sit in.

"I thought that we should keep everything out in the open," he said. "If anyone began to notice you were coming to my house every day, they might think something unto-ward was happening."

She nodded and appreciated his foresight on the matter. She sat in the chair and held very still. "How should I hold my head?" she asked.

He shook his head as he began to mix his paints. "Do not worry," he said. "You don't need to hold still. I don't paint that way. Just move however it is natural."

"Then why do you need me to sit for you?" she asked, crossing her arms in feigned annoyance.

"Is it wrong that I just want your company?" he asked innocently.

She could feel her face blush, so she looked away. "Is it wrong that I only want to be in your company as well?" she asked, unable to look him in the face.

She heard him put his painting things down and walk to her side. "Isoline," he said as he took her hand, then tilted her face to look at him. "There is no wrong here. Only love."

"Oh, Auberon," she gasped, but he quieted her with a kiss. It was a kiss of hunger and need. As If he had desired her for days without measure and could finally devour her without restraint. He nearly growled with passion as he held her tight, groping her with impunity. She was shocked by the near vulgarity of it. So much for preserving her repu-tation should someone be watching. But she met his every kiss, his every move with equal need. Her night with the man in her dreams had not been nearly as passionate as this. She wanted to tear off his clothes and climb upon him like some wild thing.

"I love you, Isoline," he gasped. "Have only ever loved you." He moved to her neck. Kissing. Tasting.

"Oh, Auberon," she panted. She could not yet say she loved him. In this moment, only lust filled her mind.

He moaned as she said his name, and then he removed her arms from around him and pushed her back, holding her at arm's length. They were both breathing hard, and she saw his eyes were eager with desire. He finally released her as he turned away. He paced for a moment in frustration, running his fingers through his hair.

"Forgive me, dear Isoline," he finally said, turning back to her after he had regained his composure. "I...I should not have done that. I am nothing but a dishonorable cad to have taken advantage of you like that."

"How dare you!" she said, feeling great offense at his words. "You think I would have let you touch me like that if I did not want it? I'm not a girl of easy virtue. I care for you, Auberon."

"And I you!" he said, rushing to take her hands in his again. "Forgive me. I did not mean to offend. I only meant that I should not have done that. If we wish to marry, everything must be proper."

"You...you wish to marry me, then?" Isoline asked. "So quickly? We barely know each other."

"I know all I need to know," he said. "I know that I cannot let you slip away from me. I need you, Isoline."

She knew that loving Auberon, wanting to marry him was reckless. Foolish. Dangerous. She hardly knew him. Knew nothing of his situation. Knew her father would never approve. Knew that her aunt would have her tossed out if she heard of her wonton ways. And yet she could not resist him. As long as she had Auberon, nothing else mattered.

"What will we do now?" she asked. "I fear we have made quite a mistake in falling for each other. My father will never give us permission to marry. All he cares about is status and title."

"I suppose that if you were to become a great heiress," Auberon said, "he might not care who you marry."

The hairs on the back of her neck bristled. "You think I should try to get money out of my aunt as well?" she asked as she walked to the chair and crossed her arms.

"Isoline," he nearly scolded, then waved his arm out over the view. "Who needs money when I have this. I should ask you if you would be willing to give up life in the big house, with servants and rich food and fancy carriages, to live in a little shack with me?"

"Of course I would!" she said. "I don't want or need any of those things. I hate the idea of trying to get an inheritance from my aunt. I only want to help care for her, be her true companion. I never came her for the money. It was my father's idea."

"Then give him all the money if you get it," he said. "We don't need it. Only each other. But if you give it to him, we can ask only for his blessing in return."

She laughed. "It would be quite a price to pay for a marriage."

He kneeled before her and took her hand. "It would be worth it," he said.

She sighed and realized that the inheritance was probably the only way she could guarantee her father's blessing.

"Very well," she said. "I will try to soften my aunt's heart toward me."

hat evening, as Isoline and Bellamira were finishing dinner, Isoline invited her aunt to a game of cards instead of retiring to their separate rooms.

"Oh, I'm sure you don't want to spend your evening with a boring old woman like me," Bellamira said.

"But I do," Isoline said. "It is not only the reason I'm here, to spend time with you, but I enjoy it."

Bellamira sat back in her chair for a moment, as if pondering Isoline's words.

"Besides," Isoline said with a smile, "who else am I going to spend the evening with?"

"Isoline," her aunt said with a sigh, "I do not wish for you to be lonely—"

"Oh, aunt," Isoline interrupted. "I didn't mean that. I wasn't *blaming* you—"

Bellamira held up her hand to stop Isoline's prattling. "I know how you meant it, dear. But I feel I must explain. I have lived here for many, many years. And for most of those years I have been blessed to not have a husband. As such, I have had the freedom to...to become the person I wish to be, not the one I was expected to be. How I look, how I act, what I believe, whom I associate with. It is all a carefully crafted identity. It is why I despise gossip. That those thoughtless chittering birds in town should have a say in how I am perceived. Well, it rattles me to no end."

Isoline nodded as she took her aunt's words in. "I'm so sorry for any role I played in causing you embarrassment," she said.

"I know," Bellamira said. "And I know that life here—in the country, in a different county, in my house—is all very different from the life you knew before. I just haven't had to...to train someone in how to behave in...well in ever. I didn't raise children up to be good little lords and ladies. I wouldn't even know where to begin to teach you how to act."

"Hopefully I don't need *too* much training," Isoline said with a chuckle. "I did have a governess after all. And a mother."

Bellamira laughed as well. "No, it's not you, my dear. It's me. I haven't the foggiest idea of what to do with you. I've never had a *companion* before. Much less an h...a niece."

Isoline nodded congenially and did her best to ignore the fact that Bellamira nearly called her an heir.

"Well, aunt," Isoline said. "I will do my best to be more patient with you if you will be more patient with me."

Bellamira nodded. "It's a deal."

CHAPTER THIRTEEN

"*N*ow this young lady," Bellamira said as she and Isoline stood before a painting of a woman with dark red hair in clothes from perhaps the reign of King James I, "was the wife of the second son of the second Earl of Payne. I believe she was of Scottish descent. I remember one of my husband's aunts saying that she had a name that sounded Scottish anyway. Emelia? Fenelia? Something like that."

Isoline nodded as she wrote a description of the painting and anything Bellamira could remember about the woman in her notebook. Isoline and Bellamira had been spending more time together and decided they needed something to occupy their time besides playing cards. Bellamira remarked that she had noticed that Isoline had not been spending as much time with the paintings as she had thought she would. Isoline admitted this was true and told her that she found the large house, empty rooms, and endless stacks of art rather daunting on her own. So every day, Bellamira came downstairs and joined Isoline for breakfast. Then they spent a couple of hours admiring and cataloging the thousands of paintings stored in the house. After luncheon, Bellamira would return to her room for a rest, and Isoline would go for a walk, which would inevitably lead her to Auberon's cottage where she would sit for his portrait between stolen kisses.

The next painting was a completely different style from the rest. It showed a woman with dark skin and free-flowing black hair dancing, waving her four arms, kicking one of her feet. She was wearing a short golden skirt and layers of gold bracelets and necklaces. She was standing before a blue background but was surrounded by a golden halo. Two of her hands were partly closed, with two of the fingers touching the thumbs. But in the hands that were open, there were large green eyes.

"This is fascinating," Isoline said. "Where is it from? Who is she?"

Bellamira stared at the painting for a moment, as though trying to remember. Isoline had noticed that Bellamira seemed to take longer to recall information as the days had passed, and she wondered if having to remember so much information was causing her to become overtired. She thought maybe she should suggest they take a few days off from their cataloging and rest.

"Hindustan," Bellamira finally said. "It's from Hindustan. I can't remember her name, but I suppose it doesn't matter. One of their pagan goddesses."

"She's beautiful," Isoline said. "I wonder what she was the goddess of."

"The night," Bellamira said. "See the yellow shining around her? That's moonlight. And the eyes in her hands. Those represent dreams, the things we see while sleeping."

"Dreams?" Isoline asked a bit too quickly. "She a goddess of dreams?"

"Dreaming, sleeping, night owls, stars," Bellamira said. "Things to do with the night."

"Fascinating," Isoline said, admiring the painting even more now. She started a new page in her book just for the description of this painting. "I shall put a star by this one. Mark it among my favorites."

"Hmm," Bellamira said as she pressed her lips into a thin line. "You do have quite a preoccupation with dreams."

"I don't hide it or deny it," Isoline said. "I've always been fascinated by dreams."

"You should be careful, my dear," Bellamira said, "not to spend too much energy dreaming. The world is...an unkind place for women. Time spent dreaming is often time wasted."

"What do you mean?" Isoline asked, looking up from her book.

"Young women dream of the perfect life, the perfect husband, the perfect home," Bellamira said, shaking her head as she left the room. "But life is not a dream. Dreams rarely come true. We must follow our duty, what is expected of us. Leave the dreaming behind."

Isoline was confused. Was she not doing her duty by being here with her aunt? "I harbor no dreams for myself," Isoline said, though she lacked conviction as she spoke. "I am content where I am."

"But your father might not be," Bellamira said.

"My father?" Isoline asked, suddenly concerned. "I have not had so much as a letter from him since my arrival."

"Well, he has written to me," Bellamira said as they walked up the stairs toward her room. "Of course, his words were all pleasantries. But I could see through them. He wants to know if you have met any eligible young men or if I had any other thoughts of your future."

"What did you tell him?" Isoline asked anxiously.

"Nothing yet," Bellamira replied. "You were supposed to be my companion. Why would I be trying to find you a husband?"

Isoline sighed. For a moment, she had been afraid that Bellamira had seen through her father's not-so subtle attempt to ask if she had considered naming Isoline as her heir. But it seemed as though the thought had not crossed Bellamira's mind.

"I am sure my father is just concerned for my well-being, as any father would be," Isoline said. "But you needn't worry. I'm perfectly happy with how things are right now."

"I hope so," Bellamira said. "I enjoy your company, Isoline. And I'm not of a mind to change a thing."

With that, she retired to her rooms for the afternoon, shutting her door.

Isoline was left alone in the hallway to ponder over her aunt's words. She was glad her aunt seemed happy to have her as a companion, but what did she mean when she said she wouldn't change a thing. Of course, her immediate thought was that Bellamira was not interested in changing her will. Isoline felt guilty for having such a thought, but what else could she have been referring to? Why didn't she want to name Isoline as heir? Had Isoline displeased her in some way? She didn't think so. She at least hoped not. Did she know about her daily visits to see Auberon? It was very possible. They weren't hiding, but were clearly out in the open. But if her aunt disapproved, why had she not said anything? Surely if she thought Isoline was acting inappropriately, she would put a stop to it. The old woman was nothing if not both vocal and proper.

Isoline sighed in frustration and then retired to her own

room to retrieve her walking boots. There was nothing she could do for the moment but wait for her aunt to speak more plainly if she was displeased. Until then, Isoline saw no reason to change her daily routine, and the thought of seeing Auberon was too delicious for her ignore.

*T*hat afternoon, as Isoline was preparing for her walk to see Auberon, the footman James knocked on her door, announcing that Tristan was in the parlor, waiting to see her.

"Did he say what he wants?" Isoline asked.

"The young lord is not of a mind to announce his intentions to a servant, miss," James bluntly replied.

Isoline stared at him for a moment, surprised by his candor. She looked to Bess, who had been helping her dress, but the frown on Bess's face seemed to convey a disapproval of Tristan, not James. Of course, the last time Tristan had been at the house, Aunt Bellamira had been none too polite about having him dismissed. She would not be surprised if the servants felt the freedom to speak their mind regarding him now.

"I know his treatment of me during his last visit was disdainful," Isoline said. "But he is still our kin, so it is our duty to show him every respect."

"Such gentility shows why you are the lady here, miss," Bess said with a genuine smile as she handed Isoline her wrap.

"I'm no more a lady than you," Isoline said as they

walked down the gallery to the main staircase. "Such titles are truly *meaningless* to me. But I suppose we should go and see what my...*cousin* wishes to say this time."

"Do you not believe he is your cousin, miss?" Bess asked. "You always seem pained to refer to him that way."

"I have technically been acquainted with Tristan longer than I have my aunt," Isoline said, recalling how he saved her from the fire and carried her home through the driving rain. "Yet he has never felt like family to me. I suppose it is because from the moment we met, his desire to make me his wife has been clearly on his sleeve. I have simply never been comfortable in his presence."

"Do you wish me to accompany you, miss?" Bess asked as she and James accompanied Isoline to the parlor. "I can, if you are concerned about being alone with him."

"Oh, I'm not afraid of him," Isoline said. "I did not mean to undermine his character in such a way. And he did save my life. But while I once wished to see him as a dear family member, I now hold him as no more than a very, *very* distant relation."

"Well, if you do require anything," James said as he opened the door to the parlor, "simply pull the cord."

Isoline smiled to herself at how protective the staff were of her "I will, James. Bess," she said. "Thank you."

When she walked into the parlor, she was surprised to see Tristan standing by the fireplace, smoking a cigarette.

"I believe grand-auntie prefers all smoking to be restrained to the smoking room," she said. "It damages the art." Indeed, the only room in the house with less than half a dozen paintings was the smoking room, and Bellamira had confided to Isoline that the pieces were so cheaply procured, the frames were worth more.

Tristan took one last long draw on the cigarette and

then tossed it into the fireplace. "Don't be a nag, cousin," he said. "It doesn't become you."

Isoline pressed her lips to stifle a retort. He was clearly not in a mood for witty banter. "To what do I owe this visit?" she asked.

"I heard about you," he said accusingly. "How you called off your engagement to Lord Crowden."

Isoline tilted her head to one side and waited. She was sure he already knew of it. It would be easy enough for anyone to know if they did any research on her. The breaking of the engagement had indeed been reported in every society page from London to York and beyond.

"Kind of funny," he said without an ounce of humor. "The day you dump a baron you end up as companion to a duchess."

"It was not the same day—" Isoline started to explain, but Tristan cut her off.

"Found a bigger fish to fry, did you?" he asked. "I bet you thought you could end up with a much larger purse playing cards with an elderly relation than by giving it all up to some minor lord."

"How dare you," Isoline gasped, truly shocked at his vulgarity. She then noticed that his hair was mussed and his shirt crumpled. He looked as though he hadn't slept in days. "Have you been drinking?" she asked.

"Only for a few hours," he said. Isoline rolled her eyes and crossed her arms. "Oh, don't you dare act so high and mighty with me," he continued. "I haven't even gotten to the best part. Not only did you leave a lord at the alter, but you've been quite free with your virtue to that worthless painter."

Without thinking, Isoline's hand flew, smacking him across the face. He reached up and held his cheek while

Isoline gasped. She immediately knew she shouldn't have done it, but she forced aside her guilt.

"I'll not allow any man to speak so of me," she said firmly. "Family or not!"

Tristan rubbed his cheek, then straightened his jacket. "You have brought so much shame to this family, should our aunt hear of it, she would most certainty turn you out."

"I have never hidden anything from her," Isoline said, her chin held high. She recalled how Bellamira actually said she had been proud of Isoline calling off her engagement. "She knows all about Lord Crowden."

"But does she know of your daily, unchaperoned visits to Dracoia's cottage?" he asked.

Isoline did not respond because she didn't know what her aunt knew of her outings. It was true that she had not spoken directly to her aunt about her visits to see Auberon, but she had not attempted to conceal them either. Every day, the staff saw her leave, she passed many of the estate's tenants, and she and Auberon worked on her portrait outside where anyone could see them. She was not surprised her visits had become known to Tristan since she had done nothing to hide them. In fact, she would only be surprised if her aunt *didn't* know about her visits to Auberon's cottage.

"That's what I thought," Tristan said, misinterpreting her silence. "She'll be furious when she finds out. You know how precious her reputation is to her."

Isoline felt her heart drop a little at that. She recalled how quickly Bellamira had turned on her when she received that newspaper clipping. Even if Bellamira did allow Isoline to occasionally associate with Auberon or speak with him about a frame or piece of art, would she approve of such regular contact? If she was truly honest with herself, she knew that she had been acting inappropriately. No guardian would ever allow a young, unmarried woman to carry on with a man the way she had.

She supposed it was possible that Bellamira had no idea about Isoline's visits to Auberon's cottage. Bellamira never left the house, never had visitors, and didn't read the society pages. Isoline knew the staff adored and protected her. It was possible they had kept the old woman in the dark about Isoline's activities.

"And you are planning to enlighten her?" Isoline asked, nervously chewing on her bottom lip.

He stepped up her quickly, grabbing her hand so tightly she was unable to pull away. "Not if you do the right thing," he said as he brought her hand to his mouth and wrapped his arm firmly around her waist.

"And what is that?" she asked as she struggled to pull away, though she already knew the answer.

"Marry me, cousin," he said, and she felt the bile rise in her mouth at his words. He held her firmly against him and tried to kiss her, but she turned her face away.

"Never!" she said, pushing him as hard as she could, but managing to move him little.

"But, Isoline," he panted as he groped her body and slobbered on her cheek. "We could have it all. We could have everything."

"I don't want anything," she said as she stomped on his foot.

He gasped in pain, loosening his grip slightly, but as she twisted to pull away, he grabbed both of her arms and turned her to face him.

"You ungrateful bitch," he spat at her. He then used his foot to knock her off balance, forcing her to the floor.

"No! Stop!" she cried, but he pulled a handkerchief from

his pocket and stuffed it into her mouth. *Pull the cord. Just pull the cord!* she thought to herself, but she couldn't even yell for help, much less pull the bell cord to get anyone's attention.

Tristan then pinned her arms together with one hand and pawed at her skirts with the other. "Don't worry, darling," he said. "After I have had you, you'll have to marry me, and then everything will be perfect, just as it was meant to be."

She wanted to cry. She wanted to scream. She wanted to get away. But she could do none of those things. She was fighting as best she could, but it was not enough. He was much too strong for her, and she was having trouble breathing with the handkerchief in her mouth. She felt herself starting to black out. There was only one person who could help her now.

Where are you? she called to the man in her dreams even though she was still awake. *Help me. Don't let him do this.*

She heard her dress rip, and she whimpered. She would never marry Tristan. If he succeeded in violating her, she would rather die than be forced to live with him as husband and wife. She tried to distract herself by imagining how she would do it. Toss herself from the top of Thornrush Manor, perhaps. Drown herself in a nearby stream like a girl in a novel? However it happened, she only hoped that she would then find herself in a perpetual dream with him, never to wake again.

"Isoline?"

Her eyes flew open at the beautiful sounds of her own name. She heard the door to the parlor open and footsteps as someone entered the room.

"Isoline?" the man said again, and she recognized it instantly.

"Auberon!" she attempted to yell with her muffled mouth.

Quicker than she could blink, Auberon was standing over them. Tristan looked up, but before he could move from atop her, Auberon grabbed him by the collar and pinned him against the fireplace.

"What is the meaning of this?" Auberon roared at Tristan.

"Come now," Tristan said with a nervous chuckle. "We were just...things were...just getting a little passionate..."

Isoline scrambled to her feet and spat the handkerchief from her mouth. She ran to the bell cord and pulled it furiously. "He was trying to force himself on me!" she cried. She suddenly felt sick in her stomach and sank into a nearby chair. It had happened so quickly. If Auberon hadn't...

Auberon snarled at Tristan and slammed him into the mantle. "You bastard!"

"Ah! Ah! Hot! Hot!" Tristan yelled as the flames from the fireplace nipped at the back of his legs.

"Get used to it!" Auberon yelled. "There will be lots of flames where you're going!"

At that, James and Talbot rushed into the room. Talbot pulled Auberon away while James attended to Tristan.

"This is no way for gentlemen to behave," Talbot scolded.

"Tristan is no gentleman!" Isoline said, her senses returning. "Auberon was only protecting me."

"Protecting?" Talbot asked, confused. "What is going on?"

"What is the unholy racket in here?" Bellamira demanded as she entered the parlor, followed by her own maid and Bess. "Mr. Dracoia? Tristan? Explain yourselves."

Bess went to Isoline's side and helped her stand from

the seat. She was shaking so hard she didn't think she could support herself on her own steam.

"I found him...assaulting Miss Isoline," Auberon explained as he paced, trying to calm down.

Bellamira's hand flew to her chest. "What? In my own home? Tristan, explain yourself!"

"It is not as simple as Mr. Dracoia suggests," Tristan tried to rationalize. "I am in love with Isoline."

"And that gives you the right to...to what?" Bellamira asked, her whole body quaking.

"I was giving her one last chance to marry me," Tristan said, pleadingly turning to Isoline. "I was trying to help her salvage was little is left of her good reputation."

"By trying to...to..." Isoline hesitated as her eyes surveyed the room. She hated to use such plain language, but she was so shaken, she needed everyone to know just how terrible the whole ordeal had been. "By trying to rape me?" she finally forced out.

Bess screamed and held Isoline tightly. James and Talbot audibly gasped in horror. Auberon tried to grab Tristan again, but Talbot shook off his shock quickly enough to restrain him. Bellamira herself collapsed onto a sofa, her maid holding her arm tightly.

"Is this true?" Bellamira whispered harshly at Tristan.

"I caught him pinning her to the floor," Auberon answered before Tristan could try and worm his way out of the situation.

"A moment of passion—" Tristan tried to say.

"With his handkerchief stuffed into her mouth to keep her from screaming for help?" Auberon interrupted, his eyes flashing in anger.

"I told you—" Tristan attempted again, but Bellamira spoke up.

"Get out, Tristan," she ordered. "Talbot."

"Yes, ma'am," Talbot replied, no further orders needed. He attempted to grip Tristan by the arm, but Tristan pulled free. He then straightened his jacket and ran his fingers through his hair. Finally, he briskly headed toward the door, Talbot on his heels.

Once the sound of the front door shutting reverberated through the house, everyone exhaled a sigh of relief.

Isoline could restrain herself no longer. She ran to Auberon and cried into his chest as he held her in his arms.

"Auberon!" she cried. "If you hadn't come when you did..." She couldn't bear to finish.

"When you didn't show up today, I had a feeling something was wrong," he said, petting her hair.

"Louise," Bellamira said, turning to her maid. "What is happening here?"

"I don't know, my lady," Louise said.

Isoline wiped the tears from her eyes and forced herself away from Auberon's protective embrace. "Oh, auntie," she said as she tried to keep herself from crying more, but she hung her head in shame. "I believe Tristan was motivated by jealousy. I...I have found myself falling in love with Mr. Dracoia."

"Found yourself?" Bellamira asked incredulously. "Quite by accident, I presume?"

Isoline chuckled at her aunt's words. "Not exactly," she admitted. "I have been seeing him regularly. But always publically! I never wanted to bring shame on you or risk my reputation."

"And how does Mr. Dracoia feel about this?" she asked, turning to him.

"I too have strong feelings for Miss Isoline," he said with a smile as he brought Isoline's hand to his mouth and kissed the back of it. Isoline felt the warmth of his lips rush through her body. She felt comforted in his presence. Safe. Something she sorely needed at the moment.

Bellamira pressed her lips and seemed to give this some thought. Isoline held her breath, afraid of what her aunt would say. While she was clearly upset with Tristan, would she also be disappointed in her niece? Was she to lose the only two kin in her life in one moment?

"So much for never wanting to marry, I suppose?" she said to Isoline with a mischievous twinkle in her eye.

"I never intended to mislead you," Isoline said, rushing to her aunt's side. "When I came here, I only wanted to be your companion. I never imagined that, here, so far from my home that I might fall in love."

Bellamira nodded. "No, I supposed you had no way of knowing such a thing before you came here," she said. "But you realize your father will never approve."

"I know," Isoline said with a sad nod. "I don't know what the future holds. I do not know if I will marry Auberon or not. If we did marry, could I be happy living in a cottage with an artist who has no desire for more in life? I don't know. But I do know that my feelings for Auberon are real, and they deserve to be explored."

Bellamira reached over and squeezed Isoline's hand. "Your words would surely be able to move even a heart of stone."

"I do not believe you have a stone heart, aunt," Isoline said with a small laugh. "I believe you have a gentle one you only try hard to protect."

Now it was Bellamira's turn to laugh. "No one has ever dared to accuse me of having a kind heart. The only woman with any softness to dwell within Thronrush Manor for two centuries has been you."

Isoline's heart swelled at her aunt's words.

"But be careful, my darling," Bellamira said. "There are many who would prey on a sweetness such as yours."

"I had no idea Tristan would turn out to be such a...a blaggard!" Isoline dared to say.

"Tristan is only one of many," Bellamira said. "Though Mr. Dracoia is not one of them. He is truly a gem among the pebbles."

Isoline looked at Auberon, who had stood politely quiet as the two women spoke.

"I believe he is one of the good ones," Isoline said proudly.

Bellamira nodded and stood, her maid holding her arm. "Then I give him permission to call on you in a more formal capacity," she said. "Though we shall keep your father in the dark for a little while longer."

"Oh, thank you, dear auntie!" Isoline said, rushing over and giving Bellamira a hug.

Bellamira patted her niece on the shoulder but then shrugged her away. "There, there. No need for such an outpouring."

Isoline released her aunt from her grip. Auberon approached and gave Bellamira a bow.

"Thank you, your ladyship," he said.

Bellamira sucked in a breath, as though she might cry. But she waved him off as she turned away. "Just keep everything above reproach," she admonished.

"We will, auntie," Isoline said as Auberon took her hand and kissed her cheek. "We promise."

CHAPTER FOURTEEN

*I*soline watched the scenery pass through the carriage window as it whizzed toward town. She took in a deep breath of fresh air and felt the sun warm her face.

"You seem to be in a good mood," Bess observed.

"I am," Isoline said with a smile. "For the first time in longer than I can remember, I feel..." She paused as she tried to put a finger on this new feeling of contentment. There had been days since she came to Thornrush Manor when she felt happy. But this was new. This was stronger. This had permanence to it. For the first time, she could imagine the future beyond tomorrow.

"Safe," she finally settled on. "I feel safe, secure. My life is not just here and now, but I feel like I can finally plan for the future."

"Even after what happened with Mr. Tristan?" Bess asked, concern knitted on her brow. "You feel safe after that?"

Isoline did feel a twinge of queasiness in her stomach at

the memory of Tristan and what he had tried to do. But she shook her head to dispel the memory.

"Tristan is gone," she said confidently. "We don't need to worry or fear him. Auntie has banished him and Auberon would do him great harm if he tried to come near us again."

Bess chuckled. "I believe that's true," she said. "He had a monstrous fury in his eyes as he held him to the fireplace. He'd do anything to protect you."

Isoline's cheeks warmed at the knowledge. She had never known such protection, such devotion from a man. Even her own father would sell her down the river if he thought it would benefit the family. She sighed and shook her head.

"Let us have no more talk or worry of men," she said. "We are going to have a lovely day."

She admitted to herself that she was a little nervous that Tristan might be attending church that day as well, but she knew that he couldn't hurt her. If he even tried to approach her, Auberon would find out about it. Isoline had asked Auberon to attend church with her, if for no other reasons but to put rumors to rest that she had been courted by Tristan. But he laughed at the prospect. "The whole world is my church," he said. "And I worship whatever I see." She had seen the way he admired the view and knew his words to be true.

But she had also sent a note the previous day to the vicar and requested they have luncheon together with his family. She hoped the opportunity would arise where she could correct any ill-conceived notions about her and Tristan. She would probably avoid mentioning her relationship with Auberon as well. No need to alert the community about something that was only just beginning. Should they become formally engaged, she be so happy she would alert the newspapers herself. But until then, she preferred to keep her new romance private.

They arrived only a few minutes before the service began—by design, so that Isoline wouldn't have to associate with Tristan should he make an appearance. But as she surveyed the congregants, she was glad to see he was not among them. Once again, she was warmly greeted by the vicar and his wife, but the rest of the parishioners kept her at a cool distance. She tried to not take this indifference personally. After all, they didn't know her or how long she would be in town. Was she merely a treasure hunter or a valuable member of the community? They probably thought it best to observe her for a while before reaching out. Hopefully, her luncheon with the vicar's family would convince everyone that she was someone worth welcoming into the fold.

As she made her way into the church and to a seat, she kept a warm smile on her face in the hopes that she would appear friendly and welcoming. A few people gave her polite nods in return, which was at least more than she received on her last visit to town.

After the sermon, she once again waited in line to thank the vicar and his wife.

"I heard she broke his heart," a voice behind her said, and Isoline new instantly they were talking about her and Tristan.

"He can hardly leave his home for the shame of it," another woman said.

"Ungrateful and cruel," another voice said. "If I could hook a handsome, respectable lord like that, I'd snatch him up without a second thought."

Isoline could not stand by silently this time and turned to face the gossiping ninnies.

"Then I wish you would," Isoline said. "Then maybe he would finally leave me alone."

For a moment, the women stood shocked into silence. But then they laughed.

"I suppose a great heiress like you doesn't have to worry about the feelings of a man like Tristan," one of the women said snidely. "Just string him along and then cut him loose when it suits you."

"I never strung him along," Isoline said calmly. "I made it clear from the first day that I would only ever think of him as a cousin."

"And what about Lord Crowden?" another woman asked with a raised eyebrow. "Did you tell him he could be a cousin too?"

Isoline started for a moment, unsure of how to respond. Of course the ladies, and everyone else in town, would know about Cyril. She just hadn't expected the incident to be thrown in her face so cruelly. It was certainly uncouth.

"Lord Crowden is a good man," Isoline said. "And I wish him the greatest happiness."

The ladies' mouths gaped like fish. They certainly had not been expecting that response. Isoline's options of what to do next flashed through her mind. Should she continue to correct them? Call them out for their nasty behavior? Offer an olive branch?

"But if you would like to know the truth of the matter," Isoline continued, "please call on me at Thornrush Manor. I'd love to host you for tea."

The ladies released a collective breath Isoline didn't realize they had been holding. They too must have been anxious about what her next move was going to be.

"In all my years, I've never seen the inside of Thornrush Manor," one of the women said as her face softened into something of a smile. "I would love to call on you, Miss Beresford."

Isoline offered her hand to shake. "Please, call me Isoline," she said.

The other ladies introduced themselves with the names Bess had told her on their previous trip, but she, of course, didn't bring up the unpleasant rumors about them she had been told. She wasn't sure how her aunt would respond to having the women in her parlor, but she would be sure to let her know in advance that they were coming so it wouldn't be a shock.

After Isoline made her way through the receiving line, she waited outside until the vicar and his family were ready to take her to their home for lunch. No one else approached her, but she watched as the ladies she had spoken to made their way around to the other parishioners, whispering what little they had learned to their friends and husbands, who then looked at Isoline and gave her a smile that was friendlier than previously. She hoped that when she returned the next weekend, the community would be more anxious to get to know her.

"*N*othing dispels rumors more quickly than the truth," Beatrice, the vicar's wife, said as she bounced a little girl on her knee.

"Perhaps," Isoline said as she finished the fish that had been served for luncheon. "But sometimes letting people believe what they want is easier than exposing old wounds."

"You don't want people to know about Lord Crowden?" Beatrice asked.

Isoline shrugged. "They will know," she said. "But I don't want to have to explain it for the rest of my life. I'm ready to move on.

The vicar and his wife laughed.

"I think that people will continue to enjoy the gossip of many subjects long after the rest of us wish they were forgotten," the vicar said.

Isoline shook her head as a housekeeper cleared away her plate. "That is surely truth," she said. "The last time I was here, those women were gossiping about Aunt Bellamira, and she hasn't left her house for ages.

The vicar poured himself and Isoline a small glass of port, but Beatrice declined.

"Your aunt is a unique matter," the vicar said. "People will always wonder about the Grande Dame living in the mansion on the hill."

Isoline nodded and sipped her drink. "I do suppose that is true. I can't blame people for being curious."

"Curious, no," Beatrice said. "But unkind, certainly. You did a lovely thing by inviting them to tea."

"I only hope they genuinely want to be friends and not just come to gawk at my aunt and her home," Isoline said.

"I think it may start out as the latter," Beatrice said honestly as she exchanged one child on her lap for another. "But let us pray it then becomes the former."

"It might take a great deal of patience on your part, Isoline," the vicar said, "to cultivate friendships in such a small community. I dare say even we struggle to find true companions."

"You must be joking," Isoline said. "I would think the vicar's family would be the social center."

"Alas, no," the vicar said. "I grew up here, it is true, but I was gone for many years to university. And I returned dragging Beatrice in tow." The two of them looked at each other adoringly. "My father...well, let's just say he had quite a reputation in town that I have yet to quite overcome."

"How do you cope?" Isoline asked. "Feeling like outcasts in your own home?"

"We do have some very dear friends," Beatrice said, taking over for her husband. "But they took many years and much patience to form. It may take a lot of work for you to be accepted here, but it will be worth it in the end."

"Marrying a local man would be the easy route," the vicar said, but his quick laugh reassured Isoline he was only speaking in jest.

"Martin!" Beatrice shrieked. "You are terrible!"

"I...I am not completely against the idea of marrying one day," Isoline said, looking deep into her goblet. "I only don't want to be pushed into it with someone I detest."

Beatrice was quiet for a moment, but she was quick to pick up on the true meaning of Isoline's words.

"Do you have someone in mind, Isoline?" she asked.

Isoline paused, but then decided to be honest. She wanted the Edwards to be her friends, and keeping secrets or misleading them would not be the way to do that.

"I...I do have a gentleman caller," she said. "Mr. Auberon Dracoia. One of my aunt's tenants."

The vicar and his wife both froze and stared at her. Then they glanced at each other uneasily.

"Your aunt..." the vicar asked cautiously. "She approves of this man calling on you?"

"Oh, yes," Isoline said quickly. "She is quite fond of him."

The Edwards seemed to breathe a little easier at that knowledge.

"Well, who am I to second-guess your guardian," the vicar said as he finished off his drink.

"You wouldn't approve if you were in her place?" Isoline asked, but the vicar didn't respond. "Please, tell me if there is anything about him I should know. He seems like a wonderful man to me, but I don't know anything about his reputation in the community."

The vicar nodded. "It isn't that he has a bad reputation," he said. "But that he has almost a nonexistent one. He's practically a hermit."

"He is a solitary person," Isoline conceded. "He is very happy on his little plot of land, free to pursue his art."

"He is handsome, wealthy, talented," Beatrice said. "You have to wonder why a man like that—one who could have his pick of ladies or live anywhere or do anything—would hide himself from the world."

Isoline's mind tripped over Beatrice referring to Auberon as wealthy. She thought he had nothing to his name but a small cottage he didn't even own. Did Beatrice know something about Auberon's situation she didn't? Or was she only assuming he was rich because of his carefree existence? She wanted to know more, but was afraid of looking ignorant if she asked. She decided she would have to ask Auberon about it directly when she saw him again.

Isoline smiled politely. "I thank you for your concern," she said. "But he is only calling. It is nothing serious yet. I have no idea what the future will hold. I only told you because I want us to be true friends. But, please, do not tell anyone else."

"Of course, of course," the vicar said. "I would be a poor

vicar if I could not keep the confidence of each one of my parishioners."

"Well, I am afraid I must excuse myself," Beatrice said as she stood. "I must put the children down for a rest."

"I should excuse myself anyway," Isoline said. "I have taken far too much of your day. But I have greatly enjoyed the company. I do hope you can come and visit me at Thornrush. We have plenty of land the children could run around on and some lovely ponies they could ride."

"Mama!" the boy cried. "Can we ride ponies?"

"Pony! Pony!" the girls chanted.

"Oh dear," Beatrice said as she watched her children quickly spiral out of control. "I believe I will now get no rest until I take you up on the offer."

"I'm so sorry," Isoline said, but she couldn't help but laugh as Beatrice and the housekeeper worked together to round up the children for their nap.

"Have a safe journey home," Beatrice said as she finally managed to wrangle her son out of the room.

The vicar laughed and followed Isoline out the door. Bess, who had taken her luncheon in the kitchen, was waiting for her with her wrap.

Isoline shook the vicar's offered hand as she descended the steps of their modest home. "I did so enjoy today. Thank you for the lovely meal and conversation."

"We must do it again," the vicar said, but Isoline could tell he wanted to say something more, so she lingered. "But...forgive me for speaking out of turn, Isoline. But I do hope you will take my—our—concerns about Mr. Dracoia to heart. Granted, I don't know the man well, and I know his family and yours go back many years. Do be cautious, though. I would hate for something to happen to you."

What exactly did he think Auberon was capable of,

Isoline wondered. If he was truly worried that Auberon was a rake, he could speak more plainly without causing offense. No, Isoline had a feeling he had some other concern, something he was afraid to give voice to.

"I greatly appreciate your counsel," Isoline said. "I will be careful and make sure every aspect of our courtship is above reproach."

The vicar smiled, but his lips were pressed tightly together. Isoline could see he was fighting the urge to say more. Finally, he nodded and shook her hand vigorously. "That is all I could ask," he settled on saying and then motioned toward her carriage.

As she and Bess rode home, Isoline watched as storm clouds gathered in the distance. Just what was the vicar trying to warn her about?

"*D*id you have a nice trip to town?" Bellamira asked as Isoline joined her in the parlor when she returned.

When Isoline saw her aunt, she nearly gasped. She looked very tired and worn. Her hair was thinner, more flat and grey. It seemed as though it was taking all her energy to sit up straight in her chair.

"Oh...yes," Isoline said, trying to mask her shock as she went to warm her hands by the fire. The storm had rolled in and Isoline's skin felt damp. "It was lovely. Thank you for asking. People were much more friendly this time. I think some of the ladies may even call for tea later in the week, if you don't mind."

"Hmm, in seventy years no one but the vicar has deigned to call on me," she said with a scoff.

Isoline nodded sympathetically. "If you would rather they didn't call, I will understand," she said. "I know you value your privacy. I could call on them instead."

"No, no," Bellamira said. "They can come. Let them gawk and stare and get it out of their system. It is those who come back for a second visit who might be interested in more than just ogling the old widow."

"You are so kind to humor me, auntie," Isoline said. "I do hope I can make friends here. Become part of the community."

"Your wide-eyed optimism will never cease to humor me," Bellamira said. She made a move as though to get up, but it seemed as though she didn't quite have a strength. She quickly recovered by turning toward the fireplace, as though that was what she had meant to do in the first place.

Isoline hesitated to inquire after her aunt's health. She didn't want to remind Bellamira about the rumors of her being a treasure hunter. But what if something was truly wrong? What if something were to happen to Bellamira? Would anyone really believe her if she said she knew nothing about her aunt's health?

"Dear auntie," Isoline finally said. "Are you feeling quite all right? You have seemed a bit tired lately."

"What?" Bellamira asked, surprised. "I'm sure I've never felt better."

Isoline nodded. "Of course," she said. But she was far from satisfied. Perhaps she should try talking to Bellamira's maid. She would know if there had been any changes in Bellamira's health lately.

"Speaking of callers," Bellamira said suddenly. "My

solicitor will be coming by soon. He's traveling up from York."

"Your solicitor?" Isoline asked. "Why will he be visiting us?"

"Just a bit of business to attend to," Bellamira said casually, as though discussing the weather. "I haven't updated my will in ages."

Isoline felt her heart bang like a sledgehammer in her chest at the mention of Bellamira's will. Of course, she didn't *say* she was naming Isoline as heir, but why else would she mention it? Isoline was too stunned to speak, so she just nodded instead.

Bellamira pushed herself to her feet and walked toward the door. "I just didn't want you to be too surprised when he came by."

"Of course, aunt," Isoline said. "I look forward to meeting him."

"I believe I shall retire for the rest of the day," Bellamira said. "This rain is seeping into my bones."

"Of course," Isoline said. "Good day."

Bellamira nodded toward her and then left the room. As soon as she was gone, Isoline nearly felt her knees give out and she collapsed onto a nearby sofa. Of course, she hadn't said it plainly, but Bellamira's meaning was clear.

She was going to make Isoline her heir.

CHAPTER FIFTEEN

Isoline laid in her bed and waited for him to come. Strangely, he had not appeared since the night of passion they shared together. It wasn't that she necessarily wanted him to appear—he always made her life so complicated when he did—she was just surprised at his long absence. The last time he had been gone this long was after she told him about her engagement to Cyril and he was angry with her. But this time, she had not told him about Auberon. In fact, they had left on good terms. Very good terms, she recalled with a slight trembling low in her stomach at the thought. She wouldn't mind a repeat of that night. One that aroused her senses to such a height she thought she would explode. She imagined that someday she would get to enjoy such passion with Auberon. But so far, they'd had to limit their intimate exchanges to stolen kisses and delicate touches. She couldn't risk bringing reproach on herself or on her aunt's house.

Especially when she was so close to being named as Bellamira's heir. At least, she assumed she would be. Bellamira had said no more on the matter, and Isoline was too afraid to ask about it. She couldn't risk angering the old woman now, not when she was so close to having everything: a man she loved, an inheritance, and being accepted by her family. She knew her father would be thrilled if he learned that Isoline had succeeded in becoming an heiress. She imagined that Auberon was probably right. That her father would be so happy he wouldn't care what she did with the rest of her life. Become an old maid or marry a nobody, it wouldn't mean anything to him. Becoming an heiress would make Isoline completely free to make her own choices in life.

And Isoline would choose Auberon.

She was so giddy with excitement at the prospect, she didn't even hear the knock at the front door.

"Mr. Lloyd Harper," Talbot announced, surprising Isoline so that she nearly fell out of her reading chair. She jumped to her feet unceremoniously and walked over to greet the man.

"I am Isoline Beresford," she said. "Lady Payne's niece."

"Miss Beresford," the man said, smiling and shaking her hand excitedly. "I have heard so much about you. I am Mr. Harper, your aunt's solicitor."

"Oh!" Isoline gasped. "My aunt told me we were expecting you, but she didn't tell me the day."

"I didn't know exactly myself," he said. "I have several clients out of York, so I try to arrange visits with as many people out of town as possible when I can."

"That makes sense," Isoline said as James walked in with a tea tray. "Can I offer you some tea?"

"I'd be delighted," he said, accepting a cup. "Now that autumn is in full swing, it can get quite nippy out there."

"Quite," Isoline agreed. "I'm from the south, so these cool mornings rather snuck up on me."

"I'm sure they did," he said, sipping at his tea. "But I gather you plan to settle in the area, so I am sure you will get used to them."

Isoline wasn't sure how to respond to that. What did he mean by settle? Did he mean stay in the area of her own accord? Marry Auberon? Inherit the estate and thus have to live here? She didn't know, and she was unsure of how to ask.

She tried to open her mouth to ask further, but nothing came out. But it didn't matter because just then Talbot returned.

"Her ladyship offers her apologies, but she wondered if she could see you in her sitting room, Mr. Harper," he said.

"Of course," Mr. Harper replied, returning his cup to the tray. "If you will excuse me, Miss Beresford."

She nodded, and he left the room quickly. No one would leave Lady Payne waiting. Isoline couldn't help but feel a little disappointed that Bellamira didn't send for her as well. After all, if they were discussing her future, shouldn't she be involved? She sighed and sat back on the sofa and waited, her chin in her hand.

As the clock over the mantle ticked, Isoline paced. Every so often, she peeked out of the room and up the stairs to see if Mr. Harper was returning, but she neither heard nor saw anything for what seemed like hours, but it could very well have been only a few minutes.

Just when she was about to go mad with waiting, she heard a door upstairs open. She closed the door to the parlor and snuck back to the sofa with her book. She didn't want Mr. Harper to think that she had been anxiously waiting for him. But he never returned to the parlor. She heard voices in the hall, but they weren't getting any closer. Wasn't he going to speak to her? Tell her if the will had been changed in her favor? Shouldn't she be told about what to expect in the future? When she heard the front door open, she could be patient no longer and threw open the parlor door.

"Mr. Harper?" she called. He looked back at her, his foot halfway out the door, his hat on his head, and his face blanched as if he had just been caught cheating on his wife.

"M-M-Miss Isoline," he finally stammered. "Do forgive me, but I simply have a mountain of work to do and must return to my office immediately."

"Oh, I'm sorry," she said. "I was only going to offer you something warm to drink before you head out."

"I only wish I had the time," he said as he doffed his hat. "Perhaps another time."

"Of course," she barely got out before he flew out of the house like a specter was on his tail. "How very odd," she muttered to Talbot as he closed the door.

He shrugged. "Lawyers usually are."

She lingered in the hall for a moment, wondering if her aunt might send for her, informing her of her sudden change in circumstances, but nothing happened. She finally returned to her book in the parlor, but she simply could not concentrate enough to read and left the book marked on the same page she had found it when she retired that evening.

"*O*h, Auberon!" she shrieked when he unveiled the painting to her several days later in the parlor. "It's beautiful! Truly!" She could not resist hugging him, she was so overjoyed with how exquisite the painting was. "I cannot believe you painted so much of this from memory."

"It is hard for me to forget your face," he said, and she blushed. He reached over and touched her cheek. "You are so beautiful when you are embarrassed."

She playfully slapped his hand away. "You are making it worse!" And they laughed. "I wonder where in the house we will hang it."

"Right across from the front door, I think," Auberon said. "That way people will always be greeted by your lovely face."

"That seems rather presumptuous," Isoline said. "I don't want to *force* people to look at me."

"I'm sure they will see it as a gift," Auberon replied.

Isoline shook her head. He was incorrigible. She leaned over to get a closer look at what looked like scribbles on the bottom right corner of the painting.

"You signed it?" she asked. "Did you think I would forget who painted it?"

He laughed. "All artists must sign their work," he explained. "Otherwise, in a hundred years, who will know who created the art with so much love."

Isoline's heart swelled. Truly, she could feel his love in every stroke of the brush he had used to immortalize her on canvas.

"I'm here, I'm here," Bellamira said as she entered the room. "James said you were insisting I come down. Well, here I am. What is so important?"

"Auberon has brought a gift," Isoline said, and she moved out of the way so her aunt could see the painting.

Bellamira did not smile when she saw the painting. In fact, her face didn't change at all.

"Don't...don't you like it?" Isoline asked. "He's been working on it for weeks."

"So, the painter has painted a painting, has he?" Bellamira asked as though annoyed. "Shall we throw him a parade?"

"N-no," Isoline stammered, confused as to why her aunt was upset. "I...I just thought you would like it. I think it is beautiful."

"It is truly one of my best pieces, Lady Payne," Auberon said with an air of humility, not boastfulness. "I had your tastes in mind as I worked on it."

"Is that so?" Bellamira asked in nearly a whisper, but she did not look at him. She stepped closer to the painting to get a better look. She stared at it for some minutes, finally reaching her hand up and barely touching what looked like the soft ruffles of the dress Isoline was wearing in it.

"What do you think?" Isoline tried again. "Where shall we hang it?"

"Get out," Bellamira said so quietly, Isoline thought she must not have heard her aunt correctly.

"Auntie?" Isoline asked. "What was that?"

"I said get out," she said again, this time with more force, and Isoline's heart dropped like a stone. Why would her aunt be kicking her out? What had she done?

"Aunt?" Isoline asked, near to tears. "What's wrong? What have I done?"

"Not you," Bellamira snapped, turning and pointing a finger at Auberon. "You! Get out!" she ordered. "I don't want to see you here again."

"Lady Payne," Auberon said with a calmness Isoline could barely understand, she was so near to tears. "Why are you angry? Is this not what you wanted?"

"What do you know?" Bellamira yelled, as much as a woman as frail as she now seemed could yell. "Thoughtless, selfish boor! Get out! I never want you in this house again!"

Auberon frowned, but finally he gave a curt bow and walked out without even a goodbye to either of them.

"Why did you do that?" Isoline asked, tears streaming down her face. "What...what did he do?"

"Never you mind," Bellamira snapped. "Talbot! Talbot, take this dreadful thing away," she said, indicating the painting of Isoline. "Take it up to...up to the princess room and lock the door. I don't ever want to see it again."

Now Isoline was thoroughly confused and scared. Why would her aunt want the painting of her locked up?

"I...I don't understand, auntie," Isoline cried. "Have I offended you in some way?"

"Your very presence offends me at this moment," Bellamira said as she followed Talbot out of the room with the painting. "I don't want to hear any more of this nonsense between you and Auberon, do you hear me?"

Isoline nodded as she followed Bellamira out of the room. "Of course. Whatever you say."

Isoline wasn't really going to give Auberon up so easily, but she would say anything at this moment to calm her aunt down. Later, she could decide what to do about Auberon. But for right now, she needed to placate her aunt enough to keep from ending up out on her own rear end. Auberon at least had his cottage to go to. If Bellamira dismissed, Isoline, she would have nowhere to go and no hope for the future.

"Just go to your room," Bellamira ordered Isoline. "I don't wish to be bothered any further tonight."

"Yes, auntie," Isoline said as she flew up the stairs to her room. "I'm sorry to have disturbed you."

She went to her room and shut the door. She waited a moment, and then peeked out to watch as Bellamira made sure that Talbot put the painting in a room down the hall—the room that had the other painting of Isoline and the one of Bellamira—and lock the door. Isoline then quickly shut her door so that Bellamira would not see her and be irritated by her further.

She sat on her bed and could do nothing but wait.

I soline...

Her eyes shot open. She must have dozed off. There was nothing else for her to do while she waited for her aunt to decide about her future. But when she sat up, she was surprised that she was still in her room, not the glade she usually woke up in when he called to her.

"...Isoline..."

She realized that it had not been his voice she had heard that woke her, but someone else's. She crept to the door and opened it slightly. Yes, someone was definitely speaking in the foyer, but she couldn't make out any of the words. She opened the door enough for her to sneak out and she crawled to the banister that surrounded the gallery.

She could hear two voices now, but they were speaking in low tones, so she couldn't make out anything more than a word or name here and there. She peeked over the top of the railing to see who it was, and she nearly shrieked when she saw who it was.

Tristan!

She felt sick to her stomach. Why would he be here? In the house? And he had been speaking to Aunt Bellamira. Why would she listen to a single word he had to say?

She knew that she should stay and try to find out what they were talking about, but she also feared that she would throw up any moment. She crept back to her room and shut the door behind her, locking it for good measure. The very idea of Tristan being in the same house as she filled her with dread.

She ran to her chamber pot and retched into the bowl. How could Bellamira trust him? Of course, she had no idea what Tristan wanted, why he was calling. Perhaps he had come to apologize. But even then, Isoline was not ready to forgive him. She did not think she ever could. He had tried to assault her, hurt her, ruin her life. He did not deserve forgiveness.

She looked up and saw a curtain flutter in the breeze. She ran to the window to make sure it was locked tight. She knew it was irrational, but she feared Tristan somehow getting into her room. As she checked and double-checked the latch, she saw something—no, someone—move in the garden out of the corner of her eye. But when she looked again, she saw nothing.

Her heart beat rapidly in her chest. Maybe it was Auberon. Maybe he was keeping an eye on her from a distance, making sure she was safe. She hoped so. She had never felt more afraid than she did right now.

She heard the heavy front door to the house close with a thud. Tristan must have left, but she couldn't know for sure. She couldn't see the front of the house from her room. She held her breath, waiting to see if Bellamira would stop by her room to talk about what happened. She hoped they could still work things out. But Bellamira did not come to her room. Neither did Bess. In fact, no one came to her room for the rest of the night. Not to help her undress. Not to bring her a meal tray. Nothing. Thankfully, Isoline did have a glass of water and a biscuit jar in her room, so she didn't starve, but she would have appreciated something more substantial to eat.

The night grew dark quickly, and there was nothing for Isoline to do except worry. Finally, Isoline undressed herself and pulled on her nightdress. She climbed into bed and laid there for hours, drifting off as the morning birds were already tweeting.

CHAPTER SIXTEEN

Isoline woke up to the sound of porcelain clattering outside her door. She rushed over and threw the door open as Bess was trying to slink silently down the hallway after depositing a tea tray.

"Bess!" Isoline whispered harshly. "What is happening?"

Bess hesitated, but then she crept back toward Isoline. "The mistress has ordered us not to attend to you," she whispered, her eyes darting around to make sure no one was watching them. "But we couldn't let you starve, so I brought you a little something. Please don't let Lady Payne know."

Isoline reached out and squeezed Bess's hand in thanks. "I won't. Thank you so much. But why is auntie so angry with me?"

Bess shook her head. "We don't know exactly. It has to do with Mr. Dracoia, but..." She seemed unsure of how to proceed.

"But...what?" Isoline asked. "She gave us her blessing. Why is she angry now?"

Bess twisted her arm free from Isoline's grip and backed down the hall. "I don't know. I can't say..."

"Well, which is it?" Isoline demanded.

Bess turned and ran down the hallway. Isoline picked up the tea tray and took it into her room. It wasn't much—toast with butter, a boiled egg, tea quickly growing cold—but it was better than nothing. She devoured the food and hoped Bess would be able to bring her luncheon as well because she knew the bit of breakfast wouldn't last long. She kept the tray in her room because she didn't want Bellamira to catch a glimpse of it in the hallway and know the servants were feeding her. How absurd! Had she really ordered them to not even bring her food?

As she paced the room, she replayed the last scene with her aunt over and over in her mind, trying to understand why her aunt had gotten so angry. It clearly had to do with the painting and Auberon. But why? Auberon had done work for Bellamira before. She was his practically his patron. It must have been because the painting was of Isoline. But...what of that? She thought her aunt had grown quite fond of her. She thought that she was Bellamira's heir. And Bellamira had given Auberon permission to call on her. She also already had a portrait of Isoline. Why was she angry over this new one?

Perhaps something had changed. For some reason, Bellamira no longer cared for Isoline or she no longer wanted Auberon to court her. Or perhaps she had changed her mind on both accounts. But again, Isoline was left with the question of why? Bellamira had said nothing to Isoline to indicate she was in any way displeased with her or Auberon. But something had to have happened. Something perhaps behind the scenes. Something Isoline had not been privy to.

She walked to the window and shivered as she took in the grey sky. She pulled a wrap around her shoulders to block the coolness that was seeping into the room. She walked over and stoked the fire, but she was out of firewood. If the servants were not attending her, the fire would soon go out and the room would get frightfully cold.

No, she could not allow that to happen. Isoline dressed herself as best she could and slipped on her shoes. She still had a key to the other rooms, and all of them had their own fireplace and stock of wood. She would simply sneak into the other rooms and pilfer the logs for her own use. She had no idea how long she would be banished, so she would take as much as she could find.

She opened the door to her room and stuck her head out into the hallway. She was surprised to hear complete silence. Usually by this time of day, the servants would be busy on their work throughout the house and could be heard cleaning, going in and out, and chattering from secluded corners. But now, the house was so silent it was as though it was empty. She realized she would have to be extra cautious. It would be too easy for her to make a noise that would alert Bellamira that she had left her room. As she entered the hallway, she pulled her door mostly closed, but not enough to click the latch. She went all the way to the end of one of the hallways, the most secluded door she could find, and carefully, quietly unlocked the door and slipped inside.

The room was like all the others—dark, unused, full of dust, and housing stacks of paintings. She squinted as her eyes adjusted to the low light, opting not to open the curtains as she didn't plan to be there for long. She shook her head at the monumental task that still lay ahead of her in cataloging the paintings if she and Bellamira ever returned to the task. If she was Bellamira's heir, what would she do with them all when she inherited the estate? It was wrong to leave the paintings locked up where no one could appreciate them. She would have to contact a museum in London to ask for advice about what to do.

She made her way over to the fireplace and found a stack of logs in a basket nearby. She grabbed the logs one at a time and piled them in the crook of her elbow, but she screamed when she felt the legs of a spider on her hand. She dropped the logs and dusted herself off of any residual spiders, webbing, or dust, then cursed herself for making such a racket over just a little spider.

She went over to the window, throwing the curtains back and taking a few deep breaths to calm her nerves. Light raindrops pelted the window and a gentle thunder rumbled in the distance. From this window, she could see the stables and the vegetable garden. Usually, even on a dreary day, the stable hands should be busy tending the horses and mucking out the stalls. But today, like the house itself, not a soul could be seen.

Where was everyone?

Even if the lady of the house was irritable and her companion shut in her room, the rest of the house should continue to function. It was as though the entire estate had simply been...turned off, for lack of a better phrase.

Isoline's despondency was changing into irritation and nearing on anger. Why should she be locked up? Even if Bellamira was angry with her, she deserved to know why. And why hadn't Bellamira told her plainly whether or not she was the heir? Why the secrets? Everyone seemed to know everything about Isoline's life and future except Isoline. She would almost prefer to being banished, forced to find her own way in the world, than live in such a state of uncertainty at the whims of everyone around her.

Why couldn't she determine her own life?

She sighed and shook her head. She knew why. It was because she was a daughter. A niece. An unmarried woman. Her life was not her own but belonged to other people. She had no choice but to live by their whims until she married —then she would be subjected to the decisions of her husband. That was the way of the world.

She stomped back over to the firewood, leaving the drapes open, and kicked at the logs and basket to make sure any linger spiders knew to bugger off. She then picked up the logs and quietly made her way back to her own room. She piled the logs on top of her dying fire and worked it until warm flames were once again roaring.

She then went to two other rooms and pilfered the logs there as well, just to make sure she wouldn't run out of wood anytime soon.

Satisfied with the temperature of her room and the pile of firewood she had accumulated, she pondered what to do next. She decided to go and have a look at Auberon's painting of her. Something about the painting had infuriated her aunt and lead her to this situation. If she looked at the painting again, more closely or with a more critical eye, perhaps she could find out why her aunt was so angered by it.

Once again, she slipped out of her room and down the hallway to the room she knew the painting had been locked in. It was the same room where she had found the rental contract for Auberon's ancestor and the paintings of her and a young Bellamira.

She entered the room and carefully closed the door behind her. The room was quite dark, as the curtains were drawn and the storm had grown even more grey. She could not see where her painting was, so she went to the window and pulled back the heavy drapes. The muted light fell on the desk. Isoline then remembered that Auberon had told her he didn't have copies of the rental contract and was unsure of his legal standing with regards to the land. Isoline opened the drawer and pulled out the papers with great care. She didn't know which ones were relevant, so she decided to take all of them. If Bellamira decided to evict Auberon from the cottage, maybe these papers could help him lay some claim to it. After all, his family had been living there for over a hundred years. That had to give him some right to stay even if the landowner wanted him gone. Isoline was far from an expert on land rights, but perhaps Auberon could consult an attorney. After collecting all the papers in the top drawer, Isoline then checked the side drawers. She didn't find anything that looked legal, but her eyes fell on a stack of letters that were secured with a ribbon. As she picked them up and turned them over, she saw only two names. On the front, they were addressed to Bellamira. On the back, they were signed from, "Your Beloved."

Isoline gasped. They must have been love letters. But from who? From what Isoline had gathered, she married young, her husband was cruel, and she was soon after made a widow who never remarried. It seemed unlikely to her that Bellamira would have had a lover anywhere in that timeframe. After all, she had been a widow for more than sixty years. She could have freely remarried decades ago. Unless the lover was a married man.

She looked at the door, as though checking to make sure it was still closed even though she had no reason to think otherwise. She knew she shouldn't open the letters, but she couldn't help herself. What if the answer to Bellamira's loneliness, sadness, and surliness toward Isoline was hidden here in these old letters?

She placed the stack of letters on the desk and carefully untied the ribbon. Her heart raced and her mouth was dry. She wasn't sure if it was the fear of doing something wrong or the anticipation of reading something salacious. Perhaps it was both. She opened the first envelope and pulled the letter out. It was yellow with age and crinkled when she unfolded it.

> *Dragă mea,*
>
>   *Even though it broke my heart to see you in your wedding dress, you never looked more lovely. I hope you do not see this as entering into a life of sadness, but hope. You are not my wife, but I will always be by your side. Dream of me tonight, and I will dream of you. One day, we will walk side by side together again.*
>
>   *Your Beloved Auberon*

Isoline's heart froze in her chest as she read the signature. She read it again and again.

Auberon.

Auberon.

No, it wasn't possible. It couldn't be *her* Auberon. This man wrote of seeing her on her wedding day seven decades ago. Her heart began to slowly beat again as she began to make sense of what she was reading. She opened the folder where she had collected the rental contracts and found a signature from the Auberon who had signed them. With a shaking hand, she compared the two. They were the same.

Of course. It wasn't her Auberon who wrote the letters, but his grandfather or great-grandfather. The first Dracoia who had come from Romania and rented land from the last Earl of Payne.

Isoline had to stifle a laugh. What a cheeky devil! Auberon's ancestor was carrying on a torrid love affair with the wife of his landlord! It was a delicious story, good enough for a novel! But after the earl died, why did they not marry? It would have been a scandal, yes, but they were clearly in love. Isoline read the next letter.

Dragă mea,

Today I saw the first bloom of spring and thought of the way your cheeks blush when you look at me. To touch your hand, to smell your hair, to kiss your lips, such sensations keep me awake at night even though I long for sleep. When I dream, then I can be with you always.

Your Beloved Auberon

Dragă mea, Isoline repeated to herself. She wondered what that meant. It was probably a term of endearment in Romanian. She would have to ask Auberon what it meant.

She then noticed the repeated mention of dreams in the letters, and she couldn't help but wonder if there was any meaning behind them. Did Bellamira have dreams the way she did? She had never mentioned her dreams to her aunt. If Bellamira ever spoke to her again, maybe she should mention them to her.

Isoline started to feel guilty about reading the letters. She shouldn't have pried into something so personal. She placed the letters back in their envelopes and tried to tie them back together, but the ribbon snapped, it was so old and delicate. She left the letters on the desk and decided she would bring a ribbon from her room to tie them with. She could have just put them in the drawer and hoped no one would be the wiser. After all, the letters had been there untouched for years. But it felt wrong to not try and put them back the way she found them.

As she headed toward the door, she then remembered that the reason she had come into the room was to look at her painting. At first, as she looked around, she didn't see it. But now she saw a painting sitting on the floor, facing the wall. She picked it up and found that it was her painting. She sighed as she looked at it in her outstretched arms. It was incredible. So lifelike! Auberon was a truly gifted painter. He could be famous if he tried. She looked around and tried to decide where to put it. Her eyes fell on the other painting of her, the one from several years ago. The one sitting next to the painting of a young Bellamira. She removed the old painting of her from the stand and replaced it with Auberon's.

Her breath caught in her chest.

She suddenly realized that not only did she and Bellamira look the same, but the art style was identical! The color palate, the brush strokes, even the dress they were wearing—everything was the same!

But it wasn't possible! Auberon couldn't have painted the painting of Bellamira. He wasn't old enough. Perhaps Auberon learned to paint from whoever painted Bellamira's portrait.

But then she recalled the signature on her painting. And on the rental agreement. And the love letters. Her heart froze.

They were the same.

She knew she had seen Auberon's signature on her painting before. And now she knew where from. She hesitated, but she knew she had to check Bellamira's painting. She had to know if they were painted by the same man.

She held her breath as she stepped forward and bent over to get a closer look at Bellamira's portrait. She saw it, clear as day.

Auberon's signature.

She gasped and stepped back. The window to the room flew open as a sharp, cold, wet breeze filled the room, scattering the love letters and the rental documents.

"Oh no!" she yelled as she tried to collect the papers from the floor. She picked up as many as she could and then ran to the desk to shove them into the top drawer before they were lost.

"What is the meaning of this?" Bellamira demanded.

Isoline looked up, and she felt ice in her veins. Bellamira was standing there in the doorway, her face hard as iron. She bent down to pick up one of the letters that had flown free, the first one Isoline had opened.

Isoline stood stone still, waiting for Bellamira's reaction. Bellamira pulled the letter out of the envelope, read it, and her face softened. She held the letter to her chest and lowered her head. Isoline thought her aunt was about to cry, and she started to move toward her from around the desk, but as soon as Bellamira looked back up, any hint of sentimentality was replaced by rage.

"How dare you!" she yelled, crumpling the letter in her hand and flinging it to the ground. "You sneak around my house, going through my things!"

"Aunt," Isoline tried to say. "I'm sorry. I was just so scared—"

"Scared?" Bellamira asked, but clearly not wanting an answer. "What do you have to be scared of? Have I not taken you in? Given you a room? Food? Clothes? And this is how you betray me? By rifling through my personal things?"

"I'm so, so sorry, aunt," Isoline tried again. "But I just—"

Bellamira stomped over to Isoline and gripped her by the wrist in a grasp so strong, Isoline was shocked into silence. Bellamira then dragged Isoline out of the room and down the hallway.

"Auntie," Isoline pleaded. "I'm sorry. Please, just talk to me."

"I'll speak to you no more," Bellamira said as she opened the door to Isoline's room and shoved her inside.

Isoline lost her balance and fell into the room. Bellamira slammed the door closed, and Isoline heard the click of the lock. She banged on the door.

"Auntie!" she cried. "What is happening? Why did you lock the door?" She shook the door handle, but it wouldn't budge.

"Just stay in there until I've decided what to do with you!" Bellamira shouted through the door, then Isoline heard her steps retreat down the hallway.

"Wait!" Isoline called out. "Come back! Don't leave me! Auntie! Bess! Talbot! Anyone!"

But there was no reply, and soon the house was once again as silent as before, save the rain on the window and Isoline crying.

CHAPTER SEVENTEEN

Isoline had no choice but to stay in her room and wait. She rubbed her wrist, which was sore from where her aunt had grabbed her and tossed her about like a rag doll. Where the woman who had seemed so old and frail lately gained such strength was beyond her. And her rage. Yes, Isoline had been wrong to snoop through her aunt's things, but the fury in her eyes gave Isoline chills. Any hope she'd had for a reconciliation with Bellamira was gone now. What was to become of her?

Her father was sure to be furious with her as well. Her chance of becoming Bellamira's heir was gone, as were any dreams of her family achieving any sort of elevated status by proxy. And what would he do with her? She was penniless and unmarried. A worthless dreg on the family resources. Would he cast her out? Send her to a nunnery? Cart her off to another distant relation? Order her to marry the next old minor lord who happened to glance her way? Every possible option seemed worse than the last.

The rain was pouring now. She could barely even see the tree in the garden. She opened the window and leaned out. There were small outcroppings of ledges here and there, but she did not imagine it would be possible for her to climb down without breaking her neck on the best of days, much less in a driving rain. Where would she go anyway? Her only friends were Vicar Edwards and his wife. And while they might be able to shelter her for a night or two, she couldn't see them housing her for any longer than that.

She sat on her bed and tried not to cry, but she felt completely hopeless.

Then she thought of Auberon. While it would be improper for him to take her in, he could take her away. They could go to Vicar Edwards and he could marry them. Bellamira would certainly cast him off the land for doing so, but they would at least have each other, and together they could figure out what to do next. She still believed he was an exceptionally skilled artist. Perhaps he could find another patron. One in London, or even on the continent! She had always dreamed of traveling to France or Italy. It would be difficult at first since they had no money...Or did they? What was it that Beatrice had said? She said that Auberon was wealthy. She never did get to ask him about that. It was possible, she supposed. He seemed to have very few expenses living in that tiny cottage. If he had saved and invested well, maybe they wouldn't have to worry about money right away.

What was she thinking? Marry Auberon? Today? Now? She hardly knew him. Of course, she *was* developing feelings for him. She didn't deny that. She would even go so far as to admit that, yes, she was falling in love with him. But was she already there? She didn't know. They were only courting, not engaged. Was she really considering marrying a man she hardly knew just to escape a bad situation? She shook her head as she continued to pace. She didn't know. If only she could talk to him. Talk to anyone! She was desperate for any amount of information. But it had been hours since Bellamira had locked her in this room and she had not heard a peep since. No one brought her any luncheon or afternoon tea, and her growling stomach reminded her of just how hungry she was.

She went to the door and jiggled the handle again, but it was still locked. She did not expect otherwise, but still had a small bit of hope in the corner of her heart that some kind soul had unlocked it. She was disappointed it was still locked, but not surprised.

"Hello?" she called softly. "Is anyone there?" There was no answer.

She dropped to her knees and perked through the keyhole. She wasn't sure what she was looking for. Any sign of human life, she supposed. After Bellamira had locked her in the room, the eerie silence of the mansion had returned.

She gasped when she saw a swish of skirts pass the door. The dower grey skirts of a maid.

"Bess!" Isoline cried. "Please! Please help me!" She waited in the quiet for a moment and was beginning to think that Bess had continued on her way when she finally heard a reply.

"I'm sorry, miss," she said. "We are under strict orders to stay away from you."

"Why?" Isoline asked. "What have I done?"

Bess did not reply, and Isoline had a feeling that Bess knew the answer to her question, but for some reason could not tell her.

"I understand you must remain loyal to your employer,"

Isoline said, trying a different tactic. "But if you can't help me, maybe someone else can."

"W-w-what do you mean, miss?" Bess asked nervously.

"Auberon," Isoline said. "You can fetch Auberon. Tell him what's happened. Ask him to help free me."

"Oh, miss," Bess pleaded. "Please don't ask this of me."

"Please try," Isoline said, feeling her only chance of escape slipping away. "I...I need you. I need him. Please help me."

Bess did not respond, but Isoline could sense she was still there. She waited for a reply, but one did not come. Finally, she heard the rustle of Bess's skirts as she turned and walked down the hall. Isoline sighed and sat with her back against the door. While Bess hadn't agreed to help, she at least didn't say no.

A small ray of hope returned to her heart.

By that evening, the rain had eased to a slow drizzle. Isoline felt mentally and physically exhausted. She was also so hungry she was starting to feel ill. But she couldn't rest. She was so anxious that if she tried to lay down, she only tossed and turned as every possible, horrible outcome ran through her mind.

But finally, she heard a click as her door was unlocked and opened.

"You are wanted in the parlor," Talbot said in his usual stoic voice, but worry was clear in the lines around his eyes.

Isoline rushed past him and into the hallway, as though

he might change his mind and lock her back in, even though Isoline knew he wouldn't dare act of his own accord and was following Bellamira's orders.

"Does my aunt wish to see me?" Isoline asked, though she didn't imagine it could be anyone else. Talbot only grimaced and motioned toward the stairwell. Isoline wasn't sure how to interpret this, but she had no choice other than to go to the parlor and see who was waiting.

"Ah, Isoline," a tall, thin man with yellow teeth said with a smile as she entered the room. "What a pleasure it is to finally meet you." He offered her his hand, which she cautiously took. It was cold and clammy, how she imagined it would feel to touch a snake. "Please, sit." He motioned toward the sofa across from him, and James brought her a teacup along with a plate of biscuits and finger sandwiches.

"Oh, thank you," she nearly gasped as she grabbed the plate from him and devoured a cucumber sandwich with one bite.

The odd man said nothing but eyed her with a curious gleam in his eye.

"I'm sorry," she said as she gulped her tea after the second sandwich. "I'm simply famished."

"No need to apologize," he said. "I hear you have had a... difficult few days."

Isoline regarded him as she ate one, two, three biscuits. "And who are you?" she asked rather bluntly.

"You may call me Dr. Shore. I'm a friend of your aunt, from York."

"She's never mentioned you," Isoline said as she slowed her eating, the food settling uncomfortably in her stomach.

Dr. Shore chuckled. "I don't think Lady Payne speaks much of her personal life, does she? Even to her own family?"

Isoline knew that delving into Bellamira's private life was part of the reason why she was in this mess. "I don't wish to discuss my aunt with someone I don't know," Isoline said.

Dr. Shore nodded. "Probably wise. Maybe you could tell me something about you."

"Me?" she asked.

"Indeed," he said. "How have you settled in here at Thornrush Manor?"

"I like it just fine," she said.

"Do you sleep well?" he asked quickly.

"I beg your pardon?" Isoline asked indignantly.

"Your dreams," he clarified. "I have heard from several people that you talk quite often about your dreams."

Who was this man and why would he have any interest in her dreams? Where was her aunt? What did any of this have to do with her current dispute with Bellamira?

"I'm sorry," she said as she stood. "I'm simply not comfortable speaking you on this matter. Please excuse me." But as she turned to leave, he gripped her arm.

"I'm sorry, my dear," he said as she tried to pull free. "But I am afraid you are going to have to come with me."

"What?" she shrieked as she continued to struggle. "What are you talking about? Who are you?"

"Your aunt and I believe your mind has become...alienated from your true nature, and that you would benefit from a stay at my facility," he explained, and Isoline felt her face blanch.

This man was a doctor of the mind. He thought she was insane and was taking her to an asylum!

"No!" she cried, somehow finding the strength to break free and run from the parlor toward the front door. It was late, dark, cold, and wet. But she didn't care. She would face all manner of hardship before she allowed herself to be committed. She would hide in the woods and then somehow make it back to her father's house. He could never stand the shame of having a daughter in an asylum.

But as she neared the door, two men in white uniforms she didn't know were standing there, blocking her escape. They must work for Dr. Shore, she realized, turning back, but Dr. Shore was in her path. She looked up the grand staircase, but Talbot and James were there. Behind them stood Bellamira.

"Auntie!" Isoline cried. "Please! I'm so sorry. I was completely in the wrong. But I'm not crazy! Don't let him take me away!"

Bellamira only frowned, her claw-like hands folded in front of her. She was starting to truly look old. Her face was wrinkled and her skin papery. She had lost so much weight her dress nearly hung off of her. What was happening to her?

Isoline heard the front door open, so she turned. "Auberon!" she cried as he entered, dripping wet from the rain. She was so happy she nearly burst into tears.

"What is happening?" he asked as Isoline ran into his arms.

"Auntie is sending me to an insane asylum!" Isoline quickly explained. "Don't let her! Help me! Take me away from this place."

"What?" he asked, holding Isoline tight as one of the uniformed men approached. "Bellamira!" he yelled, shocking Isoline by using her aunt's given name. "What is the meaning of this?"

"Stay out of this, Auberon," Bellamira snapped stepping between Talbot and James as she descended the stairs. "This has nothing to do with you."

"This has everything to do with me," he growled. "You agreed—"

"But don't you see," Bellamira said, cutting him off. "Everything has changed."

Isoline's head was spinning. What were they talking about? Why were they even talking? They should be running! She tugged on Auberon's arm. "Please, let's just go," she begged. She then felt the hand of one of the uniformed men on her shoulder, trying to pull her away. "Stop!" she screamed, trying to get away from him and back into the safety of Auberon's embrace, but as the man pulled her further from Auberon, Auberon did not try to pull her back to him!

"What do you mean?" Auberon asked Bellamira, but Isoline didn't wait for an answer. She couldn't. Both of the uniformed men were dragging her toward the door, helpfully held open by Dr. Shore.

"Auberon," Isoline shouted. "Auberon, help me!"

He let her go.

He just stood there, looking helplessly at Bellamira as Isoline slipped from his grasp and was dragged outside toward a waiting carriage.

"No, no, no!" Isoline screamed and cried as the men picked her up and threw her into the carriage and locked the door. She pounded on the window for help, but she knew everyone would obey Bellamira.

Auberon, Talbot, and James all stayed inside, not even coming outside to see her taken away. But as Dr. Shore ordered the horses to go and the carriage jolted forward, to one side of the main door, hidden in the bushes, she saw the pale face and damp red hair of Bess. She must have fetched Auberon like Isoline had asked and then had been too afraid to enter the house lest Bellamira discover her disobedience.

This one bit of knowledge, though useless to her, gave her a small amount of comfort. Maybe she wasn't completely alone in this cruel world.

She ceased screaming, but sank to the floor of the carriage and burst into tears.

CHAPTER EIGHTEEN

Isoline,

I am disappointed to hear of your current situation, but I suppose I should have seen this coming. You always were an odd girl. I suppose I overlooked your strangeness out of sentimentality, but your aunt clearly has your best interests at heart. If she thinks you would benefit from the rest, I am not one to correct her. Follow the directions of the doctors so you may get better soon and eventually return to Thornrush Manor.

Your father,

Vincent Beresford

Isoline crumpled the letter up and threw it to the floor. She held her head in despair. Always an odd girl? Whatever did he mean by that? She had always been dutiful. Could he possibly still be angry with her over calling off her engagement to Cyril? The man always could hold a grudge. She also noticed that he said she could return to Thornrush if she were released instead of returning home. Did he really think she would return to the home of a woman who had her committed to an asylum in the middle of the night after a single row? A row she didn't even understand? She never did find out why Bellamira was angry with her. And now she supposed she never would. She had been at the institution for several days and had heard nothing from her aunt. Even worse, she had heard nothing from Auberon.

Auberon.

She was more confused about him that ever before. She had severely misjudged his relationship with Bellamira. She thought he was merely a reclusive tenant that her aunt found amusing and somewhat useful. But they certainly had some sort of past relationship that Isoline had been completely blind to.

He could not have been the man who sent the old love letters or painted her portrait. It was impossible. It had to be his grandfather. But was it possible that her Auberon also had some sort of affair with Bellamira? A woman maybe sixty years his senior? She had to admit it could have happened. She had heard rumors of older widows taking young men as lovers, but never a woman of ninety! Of course, when Isoline arrived, Bellamira did not appear to be ninety, but much younger. Even now, appearing older and more frail than before, she did not show her true age. It would not be unreasonable for a woman who only appeared to be fifty should have a young paramour. It would explain why the vicar had warned her away from him, and even why Tristan had called Auberon a rake. She nearly felt sick in her stomach at the thought of Tristan possibly being right about him.

"Come now," a nurse said, leaning into Isoline's room. "Eat up already so I can clear this away."

Isoline eyed her food and dreaded putting it into her

mouth. It would be nearly impossible for her to starve here, she was fed so much and so often. Dr. Shore had told her that a stout body was key to a stout mind, whatever that meant. But the food was so coarse and flavorless it was like eating ash from an old fireplace.

She tore off a piece of the thick, dry bread and tried to slather some of the thick gruel on it, but she could barely chew it enough to make it go down her throat. She downed nearly a full glass of water just to get one mouthful of food to go down, but at least it was enough to satisfy the nurse.

"Good job," the nurse said as she took the tray away. Her foot kicked the crumpled letter from Isoline's father as she left the room. She looked down at it. "Oh, dear me. Bad news I take it?"

"My father agrees with my aunt that I need the rest," Isoline said coldly.

"Well, you will get plenty of that here," the nurse said as she left the room.

Isoline knew she meant well. Not all of the staff were as cruel and off-putting as Dr. Shore, but even though they worked here and saw the conditions, they seemed truly ignorant of what it was like to be a patient. Isoline had barely slept a wink since she arrived. The rooms were cold and spartan. The mattress was thin, as was her only blanket. She slept in her clothes to keep from freezing. The walls were thin, so the crying of those falsely imprisoned and the ravings of the truly insane crept into her mind constantly. Isoline feared that if she had not been mad when she arrived, she very soon would be.

"Was it good news?" a woman named Catherine asked, peeking her head into Isoline's room. Isoline wasn't completely sure, but she believed that Catherine was not insane, only a bit sad. She was terribly plain and had never had a serious suitor. She had no hobbies that Isoline could discern and was not particularly well educated. When her father died, instead of keeping her around as a spinster sister, her brothers had her committed. She had been diagnosed as "hysterical," though Isoline had seen no evidence of this other than a few bouts of crying that Catherine seemed to have little control over and Isoline hardly blamed her for. She had been in this place for three years.

Isoline eyed the crumpled paper on the floor.

"Oh," Catherine said when she saw it. "I'm sorry."

Isoline waved her off. "It's no matter. I knew he wouldn't help me. It was foolish to hope he might."

Catherine picked up the paper and tossed it into a bin. "Hope is never foolish," she said. "Without hope, there is no reason to keep going."

"And what do you hope for?" Isoline asked. "What keeps you from going completely mad in this place?"

"I've started writing," Catherine said a little sheepishly. "I was writing stories, but Dr. Shore would take them from me. He said they were evidence of my madness. I think he was sending them to my brothers as proof I needed to stay here. So I switched to short poems, and I've been hiding them in my mattress."

Isoline nodded sympathetically. She had a feeling that many of the "talking treatments" the doctor employed were not meant to help the inmates, but to only reinforce their beliefs that the committed should *stay* committed. Dr. Shore had repeatedly asked her about her dreams, but she had refused to tell him anything, knowing that anything she said would be reported back to her family.

Isoline leaned over and took Catherine's hand. "If I ever get out of here, I'll take your poems with me and have them published. People need to know the terrible treatment that goes on in this supposed place of healing."

"So you still have hope that you'll get out of here?" Catherine asked, surprised. "You aren't the first girl who was sent here to get her out of the way of an inheritance."

"Is that really why you think I'm here?" Isoline asked.

"Rich old dame like that," Catherine said, referring to Bellamira. "Probably has more people after that inheritance than you think."

A light seemed to go off in Isoline's head. "Tristan was at the house the night before I was taken away!" she exclaimed. "I had nearly forgotten about it. I thought he had shown up to apologize for...for attacking me. But what if he told my aunt she could easily be rid of me by having me declared insane?"

"Makes perfect sense to me," Catherine said. "My father left me money in his will. He knew I'd never marry, so he wanted to make sure I was taken care of and not a burden to my brothers. Well, guess where my money went as soon as I was locked up here."

"Oh, Catherine," Isoline said, shaking her head. "I'm so sorry."

"I'd have given them the whole lot of it willingly if it would have kept me out of this place." At that, Catherine devolved into a crying fit that she seemed unable to stop. Isoline held her friend for a long time, rocking her. She made a promise to herself, but she did not utter it out loud for fear of giving Catherine false hope. She vowed that if she ever did get out of this place, that she would devote her life to helping women who had been institutionalized.

Finally, after exhausting herself, Catherine calmed enough for Isoline to lead her back to her room. One of the nurses saw them and followed them into the room.

"What happened?" the nurse asked as she checked Catherine's pulse.

"She was just missing home," Isoline said. "As we all often do."

"Aye," the nurse said. "But no sense working yourselves up over it. It only gets your humors out of sorts."

"Have you ever been separated from your family or home against your will with no hope of ever returning?" Isoline asked in annoyance.

"Of course not," the nurse said.

"Then what do you know of it?" Isoline said more than asked.

"Get back to your room and calm down," the nurse ordered as she pulled a syringe out of her pocket and removed the cap.

"What is that?" Isoline asked in alarm. "What are you doing?"

The nurse inserted the needle into Catherine's arm, and within a moment, Catherine's eyes fluttered shut and she was unconscious.

"Catherine?" Isoline asked, going to her friend's side and shaking her. "What's wrong? What did you do?"

"Just a little something to help her sleep," the nurse said. "Nothing to concern yourself over."

"Something to help her sleep?" Isoline repeated.

The nurse nodded. "She's fine. She'll wake up in a few hours, well rested and her mind much calmer than it is now."

At that, Isoline rounded on the nurse, an idea coming to her. "How dare you!" she screamed as she grabbed the nurse's arms. "You're hurting her! You monster!"

The nurse stumbled back into the hallway. "Help! She's out of control!" she screamed.

"I'm not out of control!" Isoline yelled. "This whole place is out of control!" Then she started crying. "How could they? What is happening to me?"

She saw two men in white uniforms running toward her, and one had a syringe in his hand. She did her best to hide a smile as she continued screaming and crying.

She had been unable to sleep since she had arrived. Even though the man in her dreams had not come to her since their night of passion together, she had to believe that he would come to her in her time of need.

All will be well, he had promised her. She had never known him to go back on his word.

Isoline gasped in pain as the man inserted the needle into her arm, but she felt a warm calmness spread through her with each thump of her heart. She felt dizzy and her legs collapsed beneath her. She felt one of the men pick her up, but then the world went black.

A moment later, she was in her room back at Thornrush Manor. She sat up and grabbed her robe. As she stood, she felt the familiar sensation of wet grass under her feet. She nearly wept for joy. It had worked! And he was here with her. She could sense him.

"Hello?" she called out as she turned around, looking for him. "I know you are here. I can feel you."

Isoline...

She sighed in relief. "Yes! Yes! I'm here! I need you. Please, show yourself."

She felt his breath on the back of her neck. She turned to face him.

"Auberon!" she exclaimed. She had not expected to see anyone when she looked at him. He had never made himself known to her before, no matter how she had struggled to see his face. But she never would have believed that the man in her dreams was Auberon if she had not seen him with her own eyes just now.

"Yes, Isoline," he said. "It is me."

"All...all this time?" Isoline asked. "All these years? It has always been you?"

"Yes," he admitted, reaching out and touching her cheek. "The moment I saw your portrait, the one you sent to your aunt all those years ago, I loved you and reached out to you."

"I...I don't understand," Isoline said. "Why did you never show me your face before? Why did you not tell me when we met in person?"

"I was afraid you would not believe me," he said. "I couldn't fully manifest in your dreams when you were living at home because you were so far away. Then when I met you in person, it was like my own dream coming true and I was afraid of waking up."

Isoline searched her heart and knew that what he spoke was truth. It was him. She had the same feelings toward the man in her dreams that she did with Auberon. That was why the man in her dreams did not object to her love of Auberon the way he did of her relationship with Cyril.

"But...how?" Isoline asked. "How is this possible? What...magic is this?"

"I am not what you think," he said. "I am not like other men."

Isoline scoffed a laugh. "That is a true understatement."

"But please never doubt my love for you, Isoline," he said, grabbing her arms and pulling her toward him. He ran his fingers through her hair and looked deep into her eyes.

"Then why did you abandon me?" she asked.

He loosened his grip and shook his head. "I am so

ashamed of my actions," he said. "I will never forget the look on your face when they took you away. It haunts me."

"Then help me now," she said, stomping her foot. "Get me out of this place!"

"Bellamira," he mumbled, shaking his head and turning his face away. "She...she is still angry..."

"Forget Aunt Bellamira!" Isoline snapped. "If you love me, you will help me!"

"It is complicated, Isoline," he said, letting her go.

"Do...do you love her?" Isoline asked, her brow knitted in confusion.

"I did," he admitted. "At one time."

"Then why are you letting her control you?" Isoline asked. "What is happening? Who are you? *What* are you?"

Auberon pulled her to him again. "I will do whatever it takes to fix this," he said. "I don't know how, but I will not abandon you forever."

At that, she felt him slipping away from her. "Auberon?" she called, but the sun was rising. "Auberon! Don't leave me!" In the morning light, he faded from view.

Isoline opened her eyes and she was back in her room at the institution.

CHAPTER NINETEEN

"*I* found a newspaper clipping about you, Isoline," Dr. Shore said, offering her a piece of paper.

"If it is about me having luncheon in a public house, I've seen it," Isoline said, not taking the offered news bit.

"Oh no," he said. "This is about your accident, when you first went to Thornrush."

She didn't realize the accident had been reported in the paper, but she supposed that the near-death of a duchess's niece and presumptive heir would be something newsworthy. She reluctantly accepted the paper and read it.

The niece of the Dowager Duchess of Payne barely survived a terrible accident the night before last when her carriage fell over in a rainstorm. The girl, Miss Isoline Beresford, had apparently pulled herself safely from the burning wreckage and to a nearby tree where she was miraculously found by her own cousin, Mr. Tristan Greer.

The carriage driver did not fare so well, dying instantly in the accident. His remains have already been returned to his family.

"But I didn't pull myself from the wreckage," Isoline said. "Tristan did."

"Not according to his account," Dr. Shore said taking the clipping back. "He said that he found you in the rain, nearly frozen to death. He thinks that many of your problems might be related to your shock from the accident that you never recovered from."

Isoline sighed and shook her head. She did have some initial fears after the accident. She remembered hesitating before climbing into the carriage when she wanted to attend church for the first time. But she had overcome her fear since then.

What troubled her more was Tristan's account of the event. Why would he deny rescuing her from the fire? Wouldn't that have been an even more dramatic story? But if Tristan hadn't saved her from the carriage, then who did?

"Tell me about your dreams, Isoline," Dr. Shore asked, interrupting her thoughts as he sat across from her, a notepad on his lap, pen at the ready.

Isoline crossed her arms and refused to look at him or answer his questions. She had been inconsolable since she woke up from her dream with Auberon. He said he would not abandon her forever, but he had abandoned her for now, and that was bad enough. She was alone and scared. She had been unable to sleep without the strange injection, so she was exhausted. Even though they offered her plenty of the thick, tasteless gruel, she was starving for something satisfying. Meat, eggs, a bit of wine.

"You have read Descartes, yes?" Dr. Shore asked. Isoline tried to remain uninterested, but in her weakened state, she knew her eyes flickered. "I believe he said something along the lines of, 'I am a slave who dreams he is free—'"

"A prisoner," Isoline interrupted him to correct. She

knew she should remain silent, but she could not all this man to misquote her darling Descartes. "The original French was *prisonnier*."

"And do you feel like you are a prisoner, Isoline?" the doctor asked as he leaned forward anxiously.

Isoline chuckled. "How could I be anything else within these walls?"

"You are a guest," the doctor said. "Simply here for a short rest to ease your troubled mind."

"Why do you sit there and lie to me?" Isoline asked, her hands clenching in anger. "Even if you think I'm insane, I'm not a fool. I cannot simply walk out of here of my own accord. What is that if not a prisoner?"

"Everyone here is a patient, not a prisoner," Dr. Shore rationalized. "Once you get better, you will, of course, be allowed to leave."

Isoline pondered over this for a moment. "And what would that look like to you?" she asked. "If I were better, how would I act differently than I do now?"

Dr. Shore paused for a moment, and Isoline thought she saw a bit of sweat bead upon his brow.

"Why don't you tell me," he finally said, clearing his throat. "What do you think a mentally healthy Isoline would look like."

Isoline rolled her eyes and looked away. It was as she suspected. He was never going to release her without the consent of her father or her aunt. The doctor tried a few more times to engage her in self-incriminating conversation, but Isoline refused to take part. Finally, the doctor sighed and had one of the men in white uniforms take her back to the main sitting room where some of the better behaved women were allowed to associate. Catherine and two other women were sitting around a table playing cards and waved Isoline over.

"How did it go?" Catherine asked as she dealt everyone a new hand.

"Same as always," Isoline said. "But I think I confirmed what I already knew—that I'm never getting out of here."

"I'm sorry to hear that," Sabine, a mulatto girl who had been committed by her father's wife to keep everyone from finding out he had a mixed-race child. "At least it didn't come as any great shock to you, unlike poor Elisa here."

Elisa nodded, but didn't say anything. Isoline suspected that Elisa did have some sort of mental condition. She never spoke to anyone about anything and had been in the institution for years. Though whether she had gone mad before or after entering the asylum was some matter for debate.

"If only I could escape," Isoline lamented as she looked at her cards, but she was surprised when the other women laughed at her. "What?" she asked. "Don't you dream of escaping this place."

"And go where?" Catherine asked.

"There's nowhere safe for us on the outside," Sabine said. "We'd end up selling ourselves on the street just for a bit of crusty bread. At least we don't have to sell our bodies for food here, just endure a little touching or kissing once in a while."

Isoline felt a chill up the back of her spine and turned her head to see one of the men in white suits watching them. She knew that some of the male doctors and enforcers took advantage of the women here, but thankfully she had not been victimized yet. She knew, though, that is was only a matter of time.

"You shouldn't have to put up with that," Isoline whispered harshly. "None of us should."

"We don't have a choice," Catherine said. "We live here, or we die here. That's it."

Isoline felt sick to her stomach at Catherine's words because she knew they were true.

Her hope was finally gone.

"*M*iss Beresford." One of the men in white called her name while she was sitting, looking out a window in the common room. She looked at him, but didn't respond. "Come with me, please."

She didn't remember having an appointment with Dr. Shore today, but it was possible. All the days seemed to blur together anymore.

She followed him down the hallway, but when they went past Dr. Shore's office, she began to feel alarmed.

"Where are we going?" she asked as her steps slowed.

"Just follow me, miss," he said.

She hesitated, but the man gripped her arm firmly. She tried to pull away, but then he placed his finger on his lips to shush her.

"Don't make a scene if you want to get out of here," he whispered.

"Get out of here?" she asked, confused.

He nodded and urged her to continue following him down the hallway. They turned a corner, and he opened the door to a room she had not been in before. When she looked inside, her heart swelled.

Auberon was there.

She had to pinch herself to make sure she wasn't dreaming. All the anger, the fear, the resentment she felt melted away when she saw him. She ran to him and jumped into his arms. He held her tightly and kissed her neck, her cheek, her lips.

"You're here!" she cried through happy tears. "You're really here."

"Yes," he said. "But we must leave now, before we are caught. Come with me." He started to pull her toward another door, but she held back.

"Wait," she said. "Just like that, after what you and my aunt put me through, you think I am going to go with you?"

"I will explain everything on the way," he said. "But we must leave this place now if you want to escape."

"Escape?" she asked, alarmed. "You mean I'm not being released?"

"Of course not," he said. "I tried everything to get Bellamira to sign the release papers, but she refused. I paid a handsome bribe to that man to let me in here. But we must go now, before anyone realizes you are gone."

"But...you abandoned me," she said. "You betrayed me. Why would I trust you now?"

"I didn't..." he tried to explain, but seemed unable to find the right words. "I acted poorly. I didn't mean to betray you. I never stopped loving you. But I had a...a duty to Bellamira. I didn't want to betray her either. But she has acted so badly toward you, I realized I had to make a choice. And I chose you, Isoline. For now and always, I will forever choose you."

She felt her defenses melt away at his words. She didn't know what would happen, but she believed his words to be genuine. And going with him was surely better than staying here.

"But my friends," she said. "I need to say goodbye."

"There is no time," he said. "If you go back in there, they will know something is going on. We must leave."

She felt torn. She knew that she needed to take this chance to escape, but she felt guilty simply walking away from Catherine, Sabine, and the others.

"I must ask you something," Isoline said. "Are you...wealthy?"

He took a step back as though she had slapped him. "I thought you didn't care about money," he said.

"I don't," she said. "It's not for me. But the women here, they are suffering. If I leave them, if I go with you, would you give me money to help them?"

He sighed in relief and then laughed. He turned to her and took her face in his hands. "Even now, when your own life in on the line, you would risk your own safety for someone else?"

"I would not have survived in here without them," Isoline said. "Their friendship sustained me when I thought all else was lost."

He kissed her forehead. "I am not as wealthy as Bellamira, but you will never want for anything," he said. "And I will do what I can to help your friends *after* you are safe."

Isoline realized she could ask no more of him in the moment than that. She had to escape this place. She could not help herself or her friends from within these walls.

"Let's go," she said.

He handed her a hooded cape and led her out a side door where a carriage was waiting. She was surprised to see James there, holding the door open for her.

"James?" was all she could manage to get out, she was so happy to see him.

"I hope one day you can forgive me, Miss Isoline," he said.

She squeezed his arm as tears formed in her eyes. "Already done," she said. He gave her a small bow as he closed the door after she and Auberon were inside. As the horses lurched the carriage forward, she let out a breath of relief she thought she must have been holding since the day she arrived at this cursed place.

She looked at Auberon, and she could see a hunger in his eyes. She felt a desire flutter in her belly. She leaned over and kissed him.

"Thank you," she said.

He nearly growled with need as he held her face tightly and devoured her mouth with his. As they kissed, she realized that he truly was the man of her dreams. He was the man she had shared the night of passion with. The man who had bitten her neck...

"Who are you?" she whispered in his ear as he held her close.

He sighed, as though he had not wanted to have this conversation now but knew he could put it off no longer. He looked her deep in the eyes.

"I am a vampire," he said.

She gasped and pulled away from him. "What?" she asked. "How can that be true?" She had read about vampires in books, but never imagined they could be real.

Auberon opened his mouth and she watched as two of his teeth descended into fangs. Her heart beat rapidly in her chest, not from fear, but from excitement. From the realization of the truth.

"So you *were* the one who sent love letters to Bellamira when she was a young woman?" she asked. "When she was first married."

"I had nearly forgotten about those," he said. "I didn't realize she kept them. I thought she would have destroyed them to keep her husband from finding them."

"And you painted the portrait of her, when she was my age?"

He nodded. "I did."

"And you signed the rental agreements."

He nodded again.

"How old are you?" she asked.

"I was born in the old country in 1648," he said. That was over two hundred years ago.

"You mean Romania?" she asked, even though she knew it was a stupid question but wasn't sure what else to say.

He shrugged. "It has had many names since then."

"So that is how you came to me in my dreams, because you are a vampire?" she asked.

"I have many powers," he said. "Being able to walk in someone else's dreams is one of them, but it is not my strongest asset."

"Do you...drink blood?" she was almost afraid to ask.

"Yes," he admitted, and her heart stilled. She reached up as though to protect her neck, and he laughed. "I will not bite you if you do not wish it."

"Don't you need blood to survive?" she asked.

"Yes," he said. "But I have many willing hosts." He waved his hand toward the front of the carriage, and she knew he was referencing James and the groom.

"They let you feed from them?" she prodded further for clarification. She did not want to leave any stone unturned.

"Yes," he said. "They are rewarded with eternal youth for as long as they want it. The vampire's embrace is a gift. James is nearly seventy years old. Bess is over forty."

Isoline laughed. She knew Bess was older than she looked!

"Aunt Bellamira!" she said. "That is why she looked so young when I arrived."

He nodded, but did not respond at first. He looked pained. "Bellamira was...a special case."

"Because you love her," Isoline said.

"Because I *did* love her," he said. "I drank her blood and she drank mine. It was supposed to symbolize our eternal bond. But she was worried about the state of her immortal soul. She ended things with me many years ago. She said she wanted to die a natural death and meet God with a pure soul."

"So that is why she was aging?" Isoline asked. "She stopped letting you feed from her?"

"Yes," he said. "She broke my heart. I thought we would be together until the end of the world. But I would not let her die alone. I told her I would stay by her side until she died. But then I saw your picture. You looked so much like her when she was young. I couldn't help but fall in love with you. Bellamira found out, and she encouraged me to reach out to you. That was why I started coming to you in your dreams. When your father's letter arrived seeking a placement for you, we both agreed it was fate. That you and I were meant to be together. Bellamira knew she would die, but she wanted me to be happy after she was gone."

"So what happened?" Isoline asked. "Why did she turn on me? On us? Why did she send me to that dreadful place?"

"I don't know," he said. "She refuses to speak to me other than to say she wants everything to go back to the way it was. But I cannot take her back. I do not want to be with her anymore. I love you, Isoline!"

"But you loved her too," Isoline said. "How can I believe you don't love her anymore?"

"Have you ever had to watch someone you love grow old and die?" he asked her. She was not sure how to respond to that. She had not watched someone grow old, but she had watched her mother wither away, slowly and painfully.

"Not exactly," she said softly. "But I can understand some of what you say."

"Bellamira broke my heart," he said. "But more than that, she has spent the last twenty years torturing me, making me watch as she slowly dies and will not let me do anything to save her. The pain she has caused me, it is something that I cannot forgive. The woman I loved has already died. There is only a cruel, heartless woman in her place."

Isoline reached over and squeezed Auberon's hand. "I am sorry for your loss," she said.

He leaned over and kissed her again. He groped at her body, urging her onto his lap.

"But now, we can run away together," he whispered in her ear. "Just you and me. We will be happy and safe."

"But we don't know why she turned on us," Isoline said, pulling away. "We should try to find out, try to mend things between us. She is still my family."

"She will be angry when she sees you again," he said. "You should not return to Thornrush Manor."

"But what of Bess and the other servants?" she asked. "If you are not there, they will grow old and die."

He did not reply.

"You cannot abandon them after decades of loyalty," she pressed.

He hesitated, but then he banged on the side of the carriage. "Take us back to Thornrush," he ordered.

"Yes, sir," James called back.

"We are going to regret this," Auberon said.

Isoline pulled up her skirt and straddled his lap. He moaned as she nestled herself over his bulging manhood.

"You will never regret doing the right thing," she said.

"Are you sure you want to do this?" he asked her as he reached between her thighs and found his way through her layers of clothing to stroke her opening. "Here, in a carriage, without being married?"

She undid his belt and unbuttoned his pants. "I have waited so many years for this," she said. "Dreamed of you. Fantasized about you. Longed for you."

She kissed him and pressed her body against his. She felt his naked flesh searching for hers and her whole body shuddered.

"I want you to take me," she said. "And then I want you to bite me. I want you to make me yours."

"As you command," he said as he pushed her to the floor of the carriage and ripped open her undergarments while leaving her dress unmarred. He thrust into her, and she could not suppress her moans of ecstasy. As he filled her, there was some pain, yes, but it paled in comparison to the pure joy of having this man she had wanted, needed for so many years was finally fulfilling her every wish. Her every desire. Her every dream. She wrapped her legs around him, willing him deeper. Harder. Faster.

When they reached their pinnacle of pleasure, he roared and his fangs descended. He leaned over her and bit into her neck, and she screamed in pain and fright, but then she melted into him and held him tightly to her as she achieved her pleasure again and again.

Finally, after they were both satisfied, she curled up in his arms and let him hold her. York was hours away from

Thornrush Manor, so they did not need to hurry and make themselves presentable again, though her face did blush at what James and the groom might have heard.

She felt so safe and warm in his arms, feelings she had not felt since Dr. Shore had dragged her away many days before. She was about to drift off when the carriage hit a large rock and jolted. She gasped and remembered the horrid accident she had been in on this very road many months ago when she first went to Thornrush Manor.

"Auberon?" she asked.

"Hmm?" he asked, as though he too had been near to sleep.

"Did you save my life?" she asked. "Was it you who saved me from the fire when my carriage crashed?"

He squeezed her tightly. "I would never let any harm come to you, *dragă mea*," he said.

"*Dragă mea*," she repeated. "What does that mean?"

"My love," he said.

She sighed and nestled into his chest. "I love you, too," she said.

CHAPTER TWENTY

*H*ad she really just made love to a vampire? Isoline shook her head in disbelief, and yet she knew it was true. She had seen his fangs. He had been calling to her in her dreams for years. She had seen the evidence in his signature and paintings. She could not deny the evidence she had seen with her own eyes.

Yet it was still hard for her to accept.

How would she ever explain such a thing to outsiders? To her family? No one would ever believe her. If they didn't really think she was crazy before, they would now. Besides, she knew they would have to keep this part of him a secret. No one could ever know that vampires were real, and that one was living on Thornrush Estate. People would think he was some sort of evil monster and try to hunt him down. They would be driven away. While she still did not know all the details of what it meant to be a vampire, she knew he was not a monster. She would do anything to protect him, even if that meant keeping his secret for the rest of her life.

But how long would her life be? Bellamira had remained young looking for decades and only started to age when she stopped allowing Auberon to feed from her. Would Isoline now have a preternaturally long life since Auberon was now feeding from her? She would have to ask him later. But for now, neither of them was speaking.

They had made themselves presentable as they neared Thornrush Manor and were anxiously looking out the carriage windows, watching the dark world pass by, wondering just how the conversation with Bellamira would go. Neither of them imagined the old woman would be accepting of Isoline and Auberon's love for each other. Even though returning to Thornrush had been Isoline's idea, she had no idea what outcome she was hoping for other than some sort of peace with her aunt. She had been devastated when Bellamira had sent her to the asylum. Somehow, she needed to find a way to forgive her aunt for that. She didn't think she could live peacefully without at least trying.

As the pulled up to Thornrush Manor, the house was dark. It was not yet dawn, so it made sense that everyone would still be sleeping. But still, the silence was unnerving.

"Stay here, James," Isoline told the footman. "In case we need to leave quickly."

"Yes, miss," he said.

Auberon reached for Isoline's hand, but she refused it. "I don't want to anger her further," she explained. "I'm here to make amends. It might be best if I go inside alone."

He bristled at that. "I will let you take the lead," he said. "But I'll not let you go in alone. When I left her to fetch you, she was furious. There's no telling what she might do when she sees you."

At first, Isoline wanted to laugh. What could her ninety-year-old aunt do to her? But then she remembered the rough way her aunt dragged her to her room and the surprising strength the woman had after she caught her reading the love letters.

"Does feeding from someone also give them supernatural powers?" she asked.

"No," he said. "But from drinking my blood, she does have some gifts. She could never be as strong as me without becoming a vampire, but she does have speed, strength, and stealth beyond normal humans."

That explained why her aunt seemed to move so silently around the house.

"What about me?" she asked. "Since you fed from me, will I be stronger than before?"

He chuckled and tapped her nose. "Not yet. You would have to drink my blood. But it would take time for such effects to manifest."

She nodded, knowing that she would need to be cautious. If her aunt became enraged, who knew what she might be capable of.

As she opened the door, she was horrified by what she saw.

At the bottom of the grand staircase, Bess was lying in a pool of her own blood. Isoline gasped and ran to her maid's side.

Bess groaned. "My...my lady..." she whispered.

"Shh," Isoline cooed. "Don't try to speak." She saw what looked like a slash from a knife across her chest. She looked up at Auberon with tears in her eyes. "Help her!" she commanded.

His eyes were wild as he looked around the large foyer, checking for any perceived threat.

"We need to leave this place, Isoline," he said harshly.

"I'll not leave Bess!" she yelled, not caring if her aunt

heard her. "She risked everything to bring you to me. I'll not abandon her now!"

Auberon grunted in annoyance but kneeled by Bess's side. He bit into his wrist and then dribbled his blood into her mouth, which she drank eagerly.

"What are you doing?" Isoline asked.

"The blood also has healing powers," he said. "If she is not too far gone, she will recover."

"And if she is...too far gone?" Isoline asked, her eyes wide.

Auberon did not reply, and Isoline did not press him. She would deal with the consequences later. For now, she was satisfied that Bess would be safe.

Isoline stood and headed up the stairs toward her aunt's rooms. She knew Auberon would be angry, but if she didn't go look for her aunt now, Auberon might prevent her from doing so. She had to at least try to speak to her aunt.

"Isoline!" Auberon yelled after her.

"Take Bess to the carriage, then come back for me," she replied.

Auberon growled and took Bess up in his arms. Isoline headed for the next staircase and headed to the third-floor gallery. She heard nothing save a soft rumble of thunder in the distance. Her heart was beating furiously in her chest as she raised her hand to knock on the door to her aunt's rooms. Her mouth went dry when she realized her hand was covered in Bess's blood. She wiped her hand on her stomach and then knocked lightly.

There was no answer.

She turned the handle, and the door slowly opened.

"Auntie?" Isoline whispered into the room. When there was no answer, she opened the door wider and called out a little louder. "Aunt Bellamira?"

She pushed the door all the way open and saw Bellamira rocking in a chair near the window. On the floor, she saw Bellamira's maid with a stake sticking out of her chest, blood pooled around her.

"Oh...oh, auntie!" Isoline cried. "What have you done?"

"What I should have done years ago," Bellamira said as she stood. "I was a fool to think I could take Auberon back. To think everything could go back to the way it was. They are vampires! They have no souls. They have to be vanquished."

"Your maid was not a vampire!" Isoline said. "Neither was Bess! Why did you do this?"

"They are all loyal to *him*," Bellamira said, her hands clasped tightly in front of her gripping another stake. Isoline saw the silver of the weapon shimmer in the moonlight. She knew she had to be careful least her aunt turn the weapon on her.

"We are all loyal to *you*, auntie," Isoline said pleadingly, opening her hands in a symbol of peace. "You are our matriarch. I came back to make peace with you."

"After you stole Auberon from me?" Bellamira asked loudly, but not in anger. Her voice sounded heartbroken, full of despair.

"He came to me," Isoline said, her voice soft and calm. "You know this. He came to me in my dreams. I didn't even know he existed."

Bellamira sighed and nodded. "I...I thought I was doing the right thing. By him. For me. The old vicar, he seemed so sure that I was going to Hell. He didn't know that Auberon was a vampire, of course. Only that we were living in sin. He said that my only choice was to end the relationship completely. So I cast him out and stopped exchanging blood. 'Only ye shall not eat the blood; ye shall pour it upon the earth as water,' he was fond of quoting."

Isoline was aware of the prohibition on eating blood, and that was something she realized she would have to reckon with later as well. But now was not the time.

"But you felt guilty for breaking his heart," Isoline said, adding in the part of the story she already knew. "So you approved of him falling in love with me. But what changed? Why did you turn on him? On us? On me?"

"The new vicar," Bellamira said. "I didn't leave the house much. People would never understand why a fifty-year-old woman still looked like a girl of twenty. So I had never heard one of young Vicar Edwards' sermons before. Before he came to call on you, I had not realized that the God of fire and brimstone could also be one of love and compassion. Of forgiveness."

Isoline nodded. She too appreciated the more kindly version of God the vicar had introduced her to.

"So I began to realize that as long as my love for Auberon was pure, God would not punish me for it," Bellamira explained. "God would not hold me accountable for loving someone. So I tried to accept my forgiveness and Auberon's newfound love for you. But when I saw his painting of you..."

The thunder grew louder and anger flashed in Bellamira's eyes. Her jaw clenched and she gripped the stake harder.

"He never loved you, you know," Bellamira said. "He only loves me. He loves the parts of me he sees in you. I knew it when I saw your painting."

Isoline did not respond. She knew her aunt was blinded by rage and jealousy. She admitted to herself that it was possible Auberon loved the similar qualities of both women. But that did not mean his love for either of them was unreal. The time for loving Bellamira had passed. That was all. Isoline was determined to not let jealousy drive her mad the way it had with Bellamira. She took calming breaths before speaking.

"I did not come back here for him," Isoline said. "I came here for you. You are my aunt, my family. I want to make things right between us."

The room flashed brightly as lightning struck nearby. Isoline blinked. When she opened her eyes, she gasped and stepped back as Bellamira quickly moved right in front of her.

"The only way you can make things right is if you are dead!" Bellamira said as she raised her stake in the air.

Isoline cried out and stumbled backward, but Bellamira stepped toward her, bringing her stake down.

Isoline felt her breath knocked out of her as something firmly knocked her out of the way. She looked up and saw Auberon struggling with Bellamira.

"Do not do this!" he yelled as he griped both of her wrists.

"It is the only way to get you back!" Bellamira cried.

"I'll never love you again," he said. "It's over, Bellamira!"

"You'll only be mine!" Bellamira screamed as she pulled back. He must have thought that she was relenting because he loosened his grip just enough for Bellamira to pull her arm with the stake free, which she then used to try and stab him in the heart.

Isoline screamed as Auberon gasped in pain, but Bellamira had only stabbed him in the shoulder. They continued to struggle, but Auberon lost his footing and fell back over the railing to the floor below. He landed with a sickening thud.

Isoline ran to the railing and looked over the edge. She saw his legs move as he struggled to stand.

"Stay there!" Isoline yelled. "I'm coming!"

"Look out!" he said, pointing up at her. She looked and saw that Bellamira had grabbed a candlestick from a nearby hall table and raised it to swing at her. But it was heavy and unwieldy, so Isoline was able to duck out of the way.

"Auntie!" Isoline cried. "Please, stop this!"

"This only ends one way, Isoline!" Bellamira yelled as she swung again. This time she had a better handle on the candlestick and was able to strike Isoline hard in the shoulder, knocking Isoline off balance.

Isoline realized she had to get away. Bellamira had gone completely mad and was determined to kill her. There was no reasoning with her. She had to escape. She turned and ran down the hallway, grabbing each door handle she passed. If she could get into one of the rooms and lock the door, she could buy herself some time. But each door was locked!

She was nearing the end of the hallway, where there was only a large window. She was trapped!

Even though Bellamira could move at unnatural speed, she slowly stalked toward Isoline. She was enjoying the hunt, which made Isoline feel sick to her stomach. There was a small sitting chair in the hall, so she grabbed it and smashed the window. If there were ledges, it was possible she could climb down, or fall slowly enough she wouldn't injure herself too greatly.

She knocked as much of the glass out of the pane as she could and started to step out, but she felt her aunt's hand on her shoulder. Isoline turned to face her and grabbed her wrists to hold her off. Bellamira tried to push Isoline out the window, but Isoline planted herself firmly, refusing to budge.

"Stop!" Isoline cried as she felt herself weaken under the strength of the stronger woman. "Please..."

"Just die!" Bellamira growled.

We live here, or we die here. The words of Catherine, her friend from the asylum, echoed in her ears. Isoline realized she was right. Either Isoline was going to die in this moment, or she was going to live. But she would have to choose.

Isoline held her breath and said a quick prayer for forgiveness. She then shifted her weight to one side. It was a small movement, barely discernable, but it was enough to catch Bellamira off guard.

Bellamira plunged out the window head first, screaming to her death below.

CHAPTER TWENTY-ONE

"*B*ellamira Estelle Granville," Vicar Edwards said at a private funeral attended only by Isoline, Auberon, and the household staff at the family cemetery on the Thornrush Estate, "was born in 1762, and lived a long life. She lived in the grace of God, and we pray she is now walking at His side."

Isoline had asked the vicar to keep the sermon simple, but there was little more he could say than that. A widow for seven decades with no children, no friends, and no contributions to the community, there was little else for him to add.

Isoline nodded toward the gravediggers, and they began pouring dirt onto the coffin. She did not place the first handful of dirt on it herself, nor did she drop a rose there. She simply thanked the vicar for his services and headed back to the house.

Her feelings toward her aunt were complicated, and she was not sure she would ever be able to sort them out. She had sought some sort of reconciliation, but her aunt had only tried to kill her. True, her aunt was now dead. She had paid for her crime of killing her maid and of almost killing her, Bess, and Auberon, but Isoline still felt anger in her heart. She hoped it would go away with time, but she wasn't sure it would.

As she approached the house, a carriage pulled up and Mr. Harper, the solicitor, stepped out.

"Oh dear," he said when he saw her in her mourning garb. "What has happened? Who has died?"

"My aunt," Isoline said as she pulled up her veil.

His face blanched and he kindly took her hand in his. "I am so terribly sorry for your loss. I had no idea. Your aunt sent for me several days ago, saying she wished to make further adjustments to her will, but today was the soonest I could come. How tragic!"

"Indeed," Isoline said as she tried to appear heartbroken but was afraid she only appeared stoic.

"I suppose it is a good thing I arrived then anyway," Mr. Harper said. "Shall we go inside? I have the paperwork for the will with me. I could go over the terms with you."

"With...with me?" Isoline asked. "She left me something?"

"Something?" he asked with a laugh. "Didn't she tell you?" Isoline shook her head. "My dear, she left you everything!"

The world started spinning, and Auberon had to catch her to keep her from falling.

Mr. Harper laughed as he led them inside. "I do understand it must be quite a shock."

They went to the parlor and took their places by the fire.

"Talbot," Auberon said. "Some tea for the lady and our guest."

"Yes, sir," Talbot said as he left the room.

Mr. Harper sat his business case on his lap and began

pulling out papers. "I don't know why she didn't tell you. She was quite excited to finally name an heir after so many years."

"I suppose she didn't want to get my hopes up," Isoline said. "In case she wished to change her mind."

He nodded. "She instructed me to say nothing to you that day. I thought she wanted the pleasure of telling you herself. I was surprised when I received the notice to return and make further changes. But she said nothing specific, so all I know of her final wishes is what we discussed on my last visit."

"And what were those wishes?" Isoline asked as she accepted a cup of tea from Talbot.

"Her will was quite simple," Mr. Harper said handing her a single piece of paper. "She decreed that everything should be left to her niece, Miss Isoline Beresford."

At hearing the words, Isoline's eyes teared up. Only moments before, she had never imagined forgiving her aunt. But this news had gone a long way toward softening her heart. The fact that her aunt had probably meant to change her mind and cut her out of the will didn't seem to matter.

"All you need to do to accept the terms of the will is sign at the bottom," Mr. Harper said as he handed Isoline a pen.

Isoline tried to read the page, but she could not through blurry eyes. With a shaky hand, she accepted the pen and signed at the bottom of the piece of paper.

"Congratulations, Lady Beresford," Mr. Harper said.

"Oh, I thought that the title was long gone," Isoline said.

"It is," Mr. Harper said. "But you are the lady of Thornrush Manor now. I am sure no one will deny that."

Isoline blushed. She did not think she could accept

people calling her lady when she wasn't one, but she accepted his gesture graciously.

"There is one more thing I wish to discuss with you," Mr. Harper said. "Your cousin, Mr. Greer."

Isoline felt her heart beat anxiously at the mention of him. She had informed him of their aunt's death, but she did not allow him to attend the funeral.

"In preparation for making you the heir, your aunt asked me to review the estate accounts to make sure everything was in order," Mr. Harper explained. "I am sorry to report that there were some...discrepancies."

"What sort of discrepancies?" Isoline asked.

"It was your cousin who was managing your aunt's estate," he said, and Isoline grimaced. She remembered her aunt mentioning something to that effect, but she had thought nothing of it at them time. "Apparently, his parents did not own their land, but were renting. He gifted the land and an annual stipend to himself on her behalf many years ago, but she never signed off on it. I am afraid he has stolen thousands of pounds from her over the past decade, not to mention the value of the land and house."

Isoline shook her head. She was not surprised he would do something so underhanded, especially if he had ever thought he would become her heir and inherit everything eventually anyway.

"What are Isoline's options?" Auberon asked. He had sat by silently, allowing Isoline to manage her own affairs, but he must have seen that Isoline was having a hard time coming to terms with this knowledge. She nodded that she did wish to know this information.

"We could get the law involved," Mr. Harper said. "Order him to pay back the funds or go to prison for theft if he cannot. If he somehow can pay the money back, we could have him charged with fraud."

Isoline shook her head. "I am angry with him, but I'd rather put this nasty business behind us. What else can I do?"

"He has money sent from his aunt's accounts to his every month," Mr. Harper said. "I would put a stop to this immediately."

Isoline nodded.

"And we can issue an eviction notice," he went on.

"How much money does it take for a man to live on?" Isoline asked, feeling rather foolish. But as a middle-class woman who had all her needs met by her father and then her aunt, she really didn't know what life cost.

"A man could rent a small home or city apartment, and have enough money for food and necessities, for about...oh, I'd say ten pounds per year," Mr. Harper estimated.

"Then adjust the automatic payment to two pounds per month," Isoline said. "That way he will realize I discovered his scam, but he won't immediately be destitute. He can then either come clean to me and we can come to a new arrangement, or he can vacate the estate himself when he can't afford its upkeep."

"That is quite generous of you, miss," Mr. Harper said with a wry smile as took notes down of her wishes. "I will stay in town for a few days to finish up the paperwork and make sure everything is in order before I head back to York. Is there anything else you require today?"

Isoline looked at Auberon. "There is something else," she said. "Mr. Dracoia is a third-generation resident, but he has no papers. No birth certificate or anything."

"I wish to be a legal citizen so I can marry Miss Isoline,"

Auberon explained, picking up on Isoline's quickly concocted story.

"I see," Mr. Harper said without any hint of judgment. "You were born at home? Your family probably came here with the clothes they were wearing and nothing else?"

Auberon nodded. "Something like that."

"I see this quite often with immigrant families," Mr. Harper explained. "It can be difficult to prove identity in such cases, but it can be done. Is there any paperwork with your ancestors' names?"

"A rental agreement," Isoline said. "Between the last Earl of Payne and Auberon's grandfather."

"Send it to me and there should be no problem," Mr. Harper said as he packed his papers away in his case and stood. "You'd be surprised the weight the word of an earl carries in the courts, even a dead one."

"I also wish to purchase the Shore Home for the Mentally Insane," she said, and Mr. Harper raised his eyebrow. "I wish to help improve the care of the residents there," she explained.

"That...will prove complicated," Mr. Harper said. "But I am sure it is nothing that money cannot overcome. It will take some time and research. I'll have to get back to you later on that account."

"I understand," Isoline said. "I also need you to reach out to my brothers. I wish to cover any expenses for the education of my nephews, and any nephews and nieces who come along."

"I'll write to them immediately," Mr. Harper said at the door as he doffed his hat. "Good day to you both."

After Talbot shut the door, Auberon wrapped his arms around Isoline. "You can relax now," he said softly into her ear. "Everything is as it should be."

Isoline turned to him and nodded. "For now, but who knows what the future will hold."

He took her hand and kissed the back of it. "I can only promise that we will find out what that future holds together."

"I'm going to give you your land," Isoline said. "I can't imagine you would be able to continue painting without it."

"You...do not wish me to live here? With you?" he asked.

"Actually," she said. "I'd rather live there, with you."

Auberon took her face in his hand and kissed her softly, and then harder, more hungrily. "*Dragă mea*," he panted. "I will spend eternity making you happy."

He picked her up and carried her upstairs to her room.

Eternity, she thought as she looked up into his eyes. She could barely even comprehend such a thought.

But she looked forward to learning what it meant.

THE END

I hope you enjoyed *Dangerous Passions*. Never miss a new release by subscribing to my newsletter.
http://leighandersonromance.com/subscribe/

ABOUT THE AUTHOR

 Leigh Anderson loves all things Gothic and paranormal. She did her master's thesis on vampire imagery in Gothic novels and met her husband while assuming the role of a vampire online. She currently teaches writing at several universities and has a rather impressive collection of tiny hats. She lives in a small town in the mountains where she raises bearded dragons and gives them wings for Halloween. She is currently working on too many writing projects, and yet not enough.

Sign up for her mailing list and stalk her around the web to keep in touch and be the first to learn about new releases.

Newsletter: http://leighandersonromance.com/subscribe/
Facebook:
https://www.facebook.com/LeighAndersonRomance/
Twitter: https://twitter.com/LeighA_Romance/
Goodreads: https://www.goodreads.com/leighanderson
Amazon: http://amzn.to/2wAo2t9
Bookbub: https://www.bookbub.com/authors/leigh-anderson-755d218b-1d7b-4aa2-97f9-427cb3c12f98
Instagram: https://www.instagram.com/shreddedpotatoart/
Google+:
https://plus.google.com/u/0/+LeighAndersonRomance/

ABOUT THE PUBLISHER

VISIT OUR WEBSITE
TO SEE ALL OF OUR HIGH QUALITY BOOKS:

http://www.redempresspublishing.com

Quality trade paperbacks, downloads, audio books, and books in foreign languages in genres such as historical, romance, mystery, and fantasy.